LIVE BAIT

Check out this thrilling new series:

FEARLESS® FBI

FEARLESS FBI

LIVE BAIT

Francine Pascal

SIMON PULSE
New York   London   Toronto   Sydney

First Simon Pulse edition October 2005

Copyright © 2005 by Francine Pascal

SIMON PULSE
An imprint of Simon & Schuster Children's Publishing Division
1230 Avenue of the Americas, New York, NY 10020

Produced by Alloy Entertainment
151 West 26th Street
New York, NY 10001

SIMON PULSE and colophon are registered trademarks of Simon & Schuster, Inc.

Fearless is a registered trademark of Francine Pascal

Printed in the United States of America
10 9 8 7 6 5 4 3 2 1

Library of Congress Control Number 2005928492
ISBN-13: 978-0-689-87822-0
ISBN-10: 0-689-87822-2

LIVE BAIT

Gaia

Have you ever noticed how the big decisions come to you in an instant? How when the serious questions roll around, the answers are right there at your fingertips? In the moment, you just *know*. And in that one moment, everything changes.

Don't believe me? Let's use an example that's close to home: my decision to move to California after high school graduation. It would be the understatement of the year to say that I did not overthink that choice. In fact, it was a pretty spur-of-the-moment thing. After all that had happened, I needed to start fresh. I stopped off to visit my brother in Ohio, and from there I just kept heading west. See? Split-second decision. I hopped on a Greyhound, and everything changed.

Now I have a choice again. And it's not something I get to ponder extensively. A few days ago I was dismissed from the FBI on the grounds of an inability to . . . well, there's some technical gobbledygook that I'm sure you could read if you pulled my file, but the gist was that I wasn't so much a "team player." I wasn't big on the rules. Nope, my weird, combative, superhero delusions that had essentially kept me alive for my entire high school career were in fact a huge detriment here at Quantico. Here there are procedures, policies, protocol—and I've never been much for protocol. Agent Malloy knew I'd have problems with the rules and regulations. He doubted my suitability for the program right from the get-go. But he gave me a chance anyway. And then, even when I proved him wrong, against the odds he gave me yet another opportunity at Quantico.

I thanked him, obviously, but there's no way that he knew how much this second chance meant to me. Actually, it was much more than a second chance. It was probably a third chance, to be honest.

Anyway, when the FBI asked me to apply for their training program, to officially become a lunatic-terrorist stopper, I accepted immediately. I made the decision in a heartbeat and my whole existence turned on a dime.

Agent Malloy is offering me another show of faith. He's telling me he's willing—no, maybe even eager—to have me investigate Ann's murder case. Because I was there, because I was in the room with the killer, because I adhered to procedure the moment I realized something, *anything*, was going down. It's not going to be easy, working her case while also training with the rest of the new agents in training—the NATs. But I've got to do it. There's no question about that.

Quantico is the closest thing I've got to a home. All of my skills, strengths, and talents—for once I don't have to downplay them or be embarrassed about them. For once they're an asset that others respond to and admire. And for once I'm not the only would-be superhero. The other NATs, they're not like me. They experience fear. But the flip side of that is, unlike me, they're endlessly brave. And with them I'm going to learn to experience courage, to push myself out of my comfort zone, to play nice with others. I want to catch Ann's murderer. I want to catch *all* the murderers. I want to fit in here. I want to *be* here.

It's that simple. It has to be. For starters, if I'm not here . . . then where the hell am I? What else do I have?

Things are different now. *I'm* different now. I'm fitting in. I'm even making friends. And Agent Malloy is offering me another chance. Am I going to take it?

Hell, yeah.

I'm going to take it. I'm going to take the case, and train, and I'm going to redirect the course of my life. It's a no-brainer.

See what I mean? The day-to-day BS may bog us down, but the big things? Those don't need much contemplation at all.

some sort of love-hate deal

Johnny Ray's enjoyed pretty steady patronage on any day of the week, but on this particular Friday night, it was packed to the rafters. The hard-edged, gruff regulars had come to usher in the weekend with a drink (or three) and the locals were happily doing the TGIF thing. In and of itself, that would have been an impressive crowd. Tonight, however, the group of NATs filing in from the FBI training base at Quantico was nearly twice its usual size. Every last one of the trainees had come out tonight because tonight, they had something to celebrate.

Tonight, they were celebrating two of their own.

Two frothy pints of beer were slammed down onto a wooden table in front of two women. One was Catherine Sanders. The other was Gaia Moore.

"Drink up, ladies," Brad, their cheerful benefactor, commanded them breezily. "You deserve it."

He leaned across the table, high-fiving first Catherine, then Gaia. "Awesome work! You guys are totally going to kick ass on the case."

He was referring to the fact that just a few days ago, Gaia and Catherine had been driving downtown when they became aware of a break-in occurring at a local woman's house. Not wanting to circumvent procedure, they'd called for backup, then gone in to investigate. What they'd found had left them cold.

5

Whoever had broken into this woman's house—Ann's house, they later realized—hadn't wanted any of her belongings or her money. No, he had wanted her dead. And so he had killed her.

Gaia had gotten a brief look at the killer—she'd seen almost nothing, really. Just a flash of dark wool. A shadow out of the corner of her eye. Not much to go on, but it was more than anyone else had seen, although Catherine had been there as well. The two of them were on a sort of probational promotion. They'd been given temporary badges and assigned to cover this case. Ann's case. It would be a struggle to keep up with their rigorous training schedule while they were conducting an investigation, but it was something they both had to do. There wasn't a trainee alive who wouldn't have jumped at the opportunity to work a real case. And of course, there was the fact they both wanted to catch the sociopath who had killed Ann.

"Thanks," Catherine said, managing to simultaneously smile proudly and still look humble. She ran her fingers through her short black hair, lifted her pint glass, and tilted it in Brad's direction, silently toasting him before taking a sip. He waved and went back to where his friends were sitting.

Catherine leaned across the table and clinked her glass against Gaia's. "Cheers. We did it. We're on the case."

Gaia managed a half smile. She wasn't in the mood to drink, though. She pushed her glass back and forth a bit and hoped that Catherine wouldn't notice. She didn't want to come across like some sort of party pooper. It *was* great news, and she was eager to nab the killer. But Gaia felt it was a little too early to be toasting their success.

The truth was, Gaia didn't share Catherine's attitude. They

hadn't done anything just yet. In fact, the only thing Gaia had done was see Ann's mangled body and press her fingers against Ann's cold flesh.

Gaia couldn't help but shudder at the memory. The "corpses" in Hogan's Alley had been difficult to look at, but the real deal? Almost impossible. Someone had nearly ripped Ann's head off her body, and Gaia wouldn't be able to congratulate herself on having "done" anything until that person, whoever he was, was officially behind bars.

For tonight, though, she'd have to put on a happy face. It was part of her new "start fresh" mantra. Quantico was a chance to be strong, confident—and *also* to fit in. It was strange but refreshing how those two categories of descriptors weren't diametrically opposed. She had a roommate with whom she held actual conversations. She had a group of friends with whom she went to bars on Friday nights. She had fellow trainees who, it seemed, couldn't stop swinging by her table tonight to congratulate her on the temporary badge, wish her luck, and drink to her success. Was this what friendship felt like? Camaraderie? Because Gaia could get used to this.

"Don't be pensive. Pensive and Friday night are antithetical concepts."

"Huh?" Gaia snapped out of her reverie and looked up to see her friend Kim peering at her suspiciously. His dark eyebrows were knit together in mock reproach.

"What? I'm not pensive. I'm fine. Better than fine. See?" She made a show of lifting her drink and beaming like a model from a Miller Lite commercial before taking a healthy swig. "Mmm, Friday."

Kim laughed, but he wasn't fooled for a minute. "You're thinking about the case. I can hardly blame you, but I think that you should really use this time to chill out. For starters, you earned it. And more than that—once you're deep into the investigation? I'm not sure how much free time you're going to have. It's going to be pretty intense."

"Is that your idea of a pep talk?" Gaia asked. She frowned.

Kim was right, though. She needed to chill while she still could. Kim's psychological prowess was staggeringly accurate. It was one of the main reasons he was here with her at Quantico, after all.

"Heard about the case. Congratulations." By the time Gaia had looked up to figure out the origin of the compliment, whoever had spoken was gone. She was dizzy. She'd never in her life been the focus of so much praise, save for college graduation day. And there had been some extenuating circumstances then, to be sure.

"It's so weird," she said, allowing herself to be borne along by the momentum of the evening and moving closer to her friends at their table. "I feel like a mini-celebrity."

"That's because you are," Kim said, ruffling her hair like a protective older brother. "You're going to crack this case and catch the killer, and before long you're going to be Special Agent Superstar." He glanced at Catherine and smiled at her. "You both will."

Catherine nodded briskly. "Damn straight."

The mood at the table was warm and celebratory, even in the face of a very real, imminent danger. Gaia let herself give in to the pull of newfound friendship, emotion, and even relaxation.

No, she could never really switch off the whirring gears of her hypercharged mind, but she could give it a post-college try. She leaned backward, basking in the moment. This feeling, this safe, secure, and, frankly, determined sensation—she had waited her whole life to experience this. "Special Agent Superstar," she said, grinning to herself. "I like it."

"Well, sure."

Gaia frowned and looked up. *Oh.*

Will Taylor sat across from Gaia at the table, offering a toothless smile that was thoroughly inscrutable. He was far too much of a Southern gentleman to ever be overtly rude, but she knew he wasn't necessarily thrilled with all the attention she was getting.

Will was good-looking, über-athletic, and charming. Unfortunately, he knew it. He'd succeeded his whole life—in fact, as a track champion, he'd come this close to competing in the Olympics—and wasn't used to coming in second. Which, unfortunately, had been happening more and more since he'd come to Quantico.

Since he'd begun competing against Gaia.

Will was friendly with Gaia for the most part, but his friendliness was tinged with an edge of distrust and resentment. It was clear that he wanted to be number one. Unfortunately, most of the NATs felt the same way. Kim, for instance, was a master psychologist, while Catherine could crack any computer program you threw her way. And Gaia?

Well, she had her own special "attributes."

Will was funny, smart, and acutely adept. In fact, Gaia was a bit in awe of him. Maybe more than a bit. But his cocky attitude was kind of a thing. He obviously had an issue with strong women, some sort of love-hate deal.

The question was, how much was love and how much was hate? After all, they'd kissed. Just the other day. Just before she'd discovered Ann's body and realized that dwelling on her feelings for Will was one luxury she might not be able to afford right now. There were bigger issues at hand.

Gaia opened her mouth to reply to Will's maybe-compliment, then closed it again when she realized she had nothing to say in response. She took a breath and tried again. "Well—"

Abruptly Will rose from the table and strode toward the front door of the bar. "You know, I'm actually mighty tired tonight," he said over his shoulder. "I guess that last obstacle course really did me in. I hope you don't mind if I call it an early one. You should have your pick of a ride home in this crowd."

A casual listener hearing his words wouldn't have assumed anything was wrong. But Gaia had a feeling that Will's reasons for leaving early didn't have all that much to do with feeling physically exhausted. It didn't matter, though. He didn't give her a chance to ask. Without awaiting a reply, he banged through the door and left the bar, not bothering to say goodbye.

Gaia leaned back in her seat again. "Right." She exhaled deeply. He was being a jerk. But she wasn't immune to his behavior, irrational as it was.

Kim raised his eyebrows questioningly and Catherine shrugged, both of them clearly not wanting to touch this thing, whatever it was, with a ten-foot pole. Whatever was bothering Will—and Gaia had a pretty good idea what it was—he obviously didn't want to talk about it. Gaia sat for a moment, contemplating this. Then she jumped up and followed Will outside.

He was halfway across the darkened parking lot when she pushed her way out the door. She almost didn't see him, weaving in and out of the dim, uneven fluorescent lighting. She heard the auto-lock feature on his car engage with a patented *boop-beep* and broke into a quick jog across the blacktop.

"Hey," she said, slowing to a trot and coming to a halt in front of him. She tried to casually catch her breath. "You're leaving?"

Brilliant, she thought. *Your interpersonal skills are truly dazzling.*

She didn't necessarily think Will warranted her effort to use her questionable interpersonal skills—storming out because she was getting all the attention was pretty infantile—yet some part of her felt compelled to try and make peace. Maybe it was because he was the first boy she had kissed since Jake. That had to count for something.

"Actually, I am."

And there it was again. He wasn't being rude—Will had never, in the (admittedly short-lived) time Gaia had known him, been overtly rude, but he sure wasn't being forthcoming. Or friendly. Or anything beyond the outermost limits of civility. He certainly wasn't behaving the way a more-than-friend would be expected to behave. Gaia paused. Yeah, okay, in addition to being a more-than-friend, he was also her colleague. They had to work together, and she wanted things to be cool between them. But what the heck was this? Was he *mad* at her? For being given a temporary badge? It was as though it was something she had done *to* him, for Christ's sake. She thought about turning right around and returning to the bar, where her actual friends were assembled. People who were genuinely supportive of her. She didn't need this.

But she stayed put. If Gaia was going to be completely honest with herself, then she *did* need this. She needed friends. She needed human connections. She needed to bother to figure out what made people tick. And for now, at least, "people" included Will.

"Is something wrong?" she asked politely, as though for all the world she had no idea what could be bothering him.

"Of course not," he said. But there was a slight edge to his typically sunny disposition, and he turned away so as not to have to meet her gaze head-on.

It occurred to Gaia that fawning over him was as much of an assault on his manhood as "beating" him was. It seemed she was damned if she did and damned if she didn't. So where did that leave her?

"You know, uh, it's really good for me, being put on this case," she faltered, feeling about as smooth as a marathoner in leg irons. "Because of how, you know, I was almost kicked out before. I think this will be a good chance for me to prove myself." She meant it, but the point was that she was trying to put a certain spin on the situation for Will. Trying to make him understand that maybe, even if they were both qualified for this task, she *needed* it in a way that some others might not. As a tactic, it felt a bit contrived. She resented being forced to go through these motions.

It looked like he was biting, though. Slowly Will turned his head to establish eye contact for the first time that evening. He ran his hands through his close-cropped hair. "I know," he admitted. "It's good news. I'm really happy for you. You deserve this."

For a moment Gaia allowed herself the fleeting hope that he really did understand, that his words of praise were sincere. That hope lasted all of ten seconds, or the amount of time it took for Will to open his car door and slide into the driver's seat. "You just watch out, though," he called out through the half-open window. "Next time it'll be me." His tone was just light enough that it almost appeared he was teasing. That was something.

She leaned forward so that she was just about at his level. "It's silly to go home so early," she said. "We just got here, like, an hour ago."

"I'm tired," he said. "Sorry."

And with that, he put the car in reverse, peeled backward, and drove off.

TWENTY-YEAR PITY PARTY

Gaia remained in the parking lot long enough to watch Will's car shrink into a tiny blur on the road. She sighed, pulling her long blond hair off her shoulders and into a messy knot at the base of her neck. She was irritated with the way that conversation had gone. Or, rather, non-conversation. The whole thing had lasted all of four minutes and had only fomented awkward tension.

Typical, Gaia thought with disgust. *Story of my life.*

In a flash, she realized that she was falling back into old habits. Negative thinking had been trademark "old Gaia" behavior. *Stop that,* she commanded herself. *You're not her anymore.*

Not "her" as in not the socially stilted freak show who hadn't known how to conduct a conversation with a member of the opposite sex. Okay, so she hadn't really had a serious boyfriend—or, well, any boyfriend at all—since Jake, but whatever. Her twenty-year pity party was over. Done. *Finito.* She had a new mantra, a new outlook, and, as of this week, a spanking new badge that was all sorts of official. She wasn't going to wallow over someone else's spontaneous inferiority complex or wring her hands and blame herself. No. She'd go by his room tomorrow, maybe try to figure out how things stood between them, but tonight, she wasn't going to obsess.

It was just . . . he got under her *skin.*

Gaia dusted her hands off against her jeans as if the gesture would excise Will's essence from her body and wandered back toward the bar. She was met at the front door by Kelly, the owner of Johnny Ray's and the closest thing the NATs had to a housemother of sorts. The look on Kelly's face suggested that she had witnessed the entire exchange.

"Don't worry, sweetie," she said, patting Gaia comfortably on the shoulder. "He'll get over it. Male ego bruises hard is all."

Gaia smiled. "Tell me about it."

"He's competitive, you knew that," Kelly pointed out. "Heck, he probably wouldn't be at Quantico if he weren't. So there are plenty of good sides to that kind of drive. But you've got to put up with his attitude when it rears its ugly head. Or you don't *have* to," she corrected herself. She arched an eyebrow at Gaia playfully. "Yet something tells me that you just might *want* to."

"Men are complicated," Gaia said simply, as though this were a subject on which she had any level of authority. They were certainly complicated to *her*, in any event. Which was why she steered clear of them for the most part. Besides, any man she'd ever brought into her life had only suffered as a result.

"They're not, really," Kelly disagreed. "It's when men and women get together that things get complicated. But if you're lucky, it's mostly worth the hassle, I have to say."

Gaia shook her head ruefully. "I'll let you know," she quipped.

Then she headed back to her table to rejoin her friends. So Will wasn't around. So what? She certainly didn't need him around for her good time.

Right?

A FINE LINE

Gaia might have had a new mantra and a shiny new outlook, but if there was one thing at Quantico she knew she'd never embrace fully, it was the food in the dining hall. She'd never been big on haute cuisine—back in the day, a chili dog from Gray's Papaya had been her idea of a New York City feast—but there was something about the watery scrambled eggs and dried-out sausage patties floating aimlessly in a succession of steam trays that nearly killed her appetite.

Fortunately, though, that appetite had a strong will to survive. She bypassed the eggs, sausages, and some questionable-looking pancakes and grabbed herself a yogurt and some fruit before joining Catherine and Kim at a table near the corner of the room.

"Hey," she said, settling in across from Kim. She gestured toward his plate, piled high with eggs and toast. "Living dangerously this morning?"

"I'm a thrill seeker," Kim agreed. "Anyway, whatever doesn't kill you makes you stronger, right?"

"We'll see," she said, raising her eyebrows. She quickly scanned the dining hall, not wanting to admit to herself exactly why she was doing so.

"He's not here," Kim said mildly, reading Gaia's mind and causing her to nearly flinch visibly in her seat. "He wanted to run some laps down at the track before we meet with the bomb squad."

Damn, Gaia thought, irritated at how easily Kim could see through her. She hastily reconfigured her facial features into what she hoped was a casual expression. "Oh," she said, shrugging lightly. "Cool."

"You know, I thought it was weird, Will leaving last night when he did," Catherine began, spearing a chunk of melon with her fork and downing it in one gulp. "But I have to say, I think he had the right idea. I'm beat. And I have a feeling the bomb squad isn't exactly going to be a picnic."

Gaia nodded. *Nothing* at Quantico, thus far, had exactly been what she would consider a picnic. But she was willing to work with bombs. Work *on* bombs. It had to be easier than guns, which were still a necessary evil to Gaia.

New attitude, she reminded herself. *Open mind.*

16

"I was thinking," she said, swallowing a spoonful of yogurt before continuing, "we should probably check in with Bishop and Malloy this morning. Before the bomb squad thing, I mean. Just to see, you know, exactly how we should proceed with the investigation of Ann's murder. I'd like to have a game plan. I think the case is going to be time-consuming. It probably couldn't hurt to have an idea of the blow-by-blow before we jump in." She paused, suddenly feeling uncertain. There was a fine line, after all, between proactivity and a sudden attack of control freak-dom. "Don't you think?"

Catherine nodded. "Definitely," she said. "You're right. I want to be on top of this thing." She glanced down at her watch. "Shoot. If we're going to go, we've got to go now. We have to be at bomb squad in half an hour." She pushed her plate away, leaving a mound of cottage cheese uneaten. "I was sick of this anyway. You done?"

Gaia took one last swallow of her yogurt. "Yup," she said, rising from the table purposefully. "Let's get going."

SPECIAL BLEND OF VENGEANCE

"Gaia, Catherine, good morning."

Special Agent Jennifer Bishop looked up from behind her desk at her two unexpected visitors. "I was hoping to see you both."

Gaia stepped forward. "We had a few questions about the murder investigation. We wanted to talk to you about how you would like us to proceed," Gaia said, suddenly feeling tongue-tied and insecure. "If there was some specific plan you had in place, before we set off on our own."

"Good thinking," Bishop said, nodding.

Gaia was relieved. She knew that the primary concerns that the agents had about her were mainly in regard to what they referred to as her tendencies toward "vigilante justice," otherwise known as her patented "kick butt now, ask questions later" policy. In all fairness, most of the scumbags whose butts she had kicked once upon a time had been thoroughly deserving of Gaia Moore's special blend of vengeance. But if she wanted to make it as an FBI agent, she knew she'd have to follow *their* policies and procedures, which often meant asking questions *first*.

"I'm glad you both stopped by," Bishop said, shuffling the piles of paper on the desk in front of her until she came up with a manila file folder. She opened the file and fished out a document. "Obviously you'll have our entire team at your disposal during the course of your investigation. Although you are trainees, your temporary badges will enable you to access computer equipment, lab services, databases, personnel . . . the works. Additionally, we've assigned two agents to work alongside you on your investigation: Agent Charles Crane and Agent Jackson Hyde. They will be working with you in a supervisory capacity and should not interfere with your investigation in any way."

She looked up at the girls, holding each of their respective gazes for a beat. "In other words, ladies, it's really your show. We'll be around, and we'll certainly be able to help you in the event that you have any difficulties, but the fact is that when we turned this investigation over to you, we did so in full."

"Yes, ma'am, thank you," Gaia said instantly. *Your show.* It sounded exciting and scary all at once.

"Now, if my schedules are correct—and I'm going to assume that they are—you both are expected at the bomb squad drill in about six minutes, no?" Bishop raised an eyebrow at the girls questioningly.

"Yes, ma'am," Catherine said, speaking for both of them.

"Well, given that it's all the way over in the north building, I'd suggest you make your way down there," she said, turning her attention back to her paperwork. Without looking up, she offered one final bit of wisdom: "Ladies, I'm sure you're both aware of the stresses involved in a criminal investigation. This case is going to be extremely demanding for both of you. Needless to say, we would not have assigned you to this job if we didn't think you'd be able to handle it. But if I were you, I'd be prepared to work like a madwoman. Both your training requirements and the case are going to need to take top priority, and neither can be given anything less than your complete attention. It's not going to be easy."

Gaia and Catherine both nodded. For her part, Gaia knew that she was determined to balance the case and the training. Both were of the utmost importance to her, so regardless of how difficult it was, somehow she was going to manage to do it all. No, more than that—she was going to do it all *well*. She was going to prove herself to Bishop and Malloy.

She was going to prove herself to . . . herself.

"Historically, the media and press have focused on nuclear bombs—that is, the hydrogen bomb and the atomic bomb—in their coverage of warfare. Threat of detonation of both of those classes of bombs lay behind much of the warfare and surrounding hysteria of the mid–twentieth century. Nowadays, the concern is connected to what we refer to as 'smart bombs,' so named because of their ability to pinpoint a target with great accuracy."

Gaia sat in the front row of desks in lecture hall C of the north building, leaning forward so far on her desk that she thought her seat might topple over. She found this topic genuinely fascinating. Judging from the looks of rapt attention etched on her fellow classmates' faces, she wasn't the only one. The back three rows in the lecture hall remained utterly empty—everyone wanted to be front and center for this demonstration.

Up until two months ago—up until the day of her college graduation, that was—Gaia hadn't given bombs all that much thought. All of the weird, violent, and otherwise shady interactions that she'd had as a young woman hadn't involved explosives. Guns, poison, illicit medical procedures? All the time. But no bombs. Not until Kevin Bender had threatened to blow her entire graduating class to kingdom come.

Quick thinking and a complete and total lack of fear had propelled Gaia to prevent any casualties that day, but she hadn't actually been able to prevent Kevin from detonating the bomb. The brief flash of light followed by a hollow sucking sound—the very opposite of the *ka-boom* factor she'd seen in action-hero movies and had therefore come to expect (if, in fact, one ever did truly "expect" to find oneself in such a situation)—those sounds and images had flooded her brain every night for weeks after the incident. That auto-replay had in large part been responsible for driving her to Quantico.

So, while she wasn't exceptionally worried about the A-bomb these days, she was keen to learn the science behind what Kevin had planted in her school auditorium. Just in case she ever found herself in that situation again and the odds weren't totally against this, now that she was a NAT.

"The majority of the bombs used by military agencies are smart bombs: they have steering fins, a small rocket motor, and advanced targeting systems. Despite this advanced technology, however, they are limited to a range of one additional half mile beyond the normal range."

Gaia's eyes were focused on the uniformed agent at the head of the classroom, but her mind was wandering. Despite her spotty, violence-spattered past, she detested violence itself. She even detested the thought of military-sanctioned violence. But that was why she was here. To prevent the need for such measures.

"Your typical suicide bomber—the bus bombers in Israel, for example—are not going to waste time with smart bombs. They're looking for maximum damage with minimum effort. For that reason, they're going to use 'free-fall bombs,' which are basically just what they sound like. They may have special targeting devices, but their accuracy is far less reliable than that of the smart bomb. Therefore they're most useful for smaller, more focused, hands-on attacks."

Attacks where the terrorist doesn't expect to live, Gaia realized with a start. *Like what Kevin was planning.*

"If, upon your successful completion of the course here, you do not go on to specialize in bomb squad, it is likely is that you will not find yourself face-to-face with any type of bomb. That said, if and when such an event does occur, statistically speaking, the bomb you are most likely to encounter will be homemade and therefore, thankfully, somewhat crude. You *should* have no difficulty identifying its various components and disassembling it in adequate time."

Agent Baxter, their instructor for the bomb-defusing demonstration, stepped back to the wall behind his podium and pulled down a wall chart that had been rolled up and pinned in place. Gaia squinted at the chart, struggling to read the diagram and to make sense of the squiggly lines that ran back and forth. Those lines basically represented the difference between knowing how to dismantle Kevin's contraption and the sucking, gaping vortex of her nightmare landscape.

Baxter grabbed a laser pointer and set to work tapping against the diagram, explaining to everyone just which part of the bomb was responsible for which part of the ultimate explosion. Gaia found herself scribbling down copious notes. She hadn't ever imagined herself going on to specialize in the antiterrorist unit, but this was interesting.

"Are there any questions?" he asked as his lecture wound down to a close.

"Actually, yes."

Gaia was surprised to hear Catherine's voice. She turned to her roommate, who was sitting straight up in her seat, thick tortoiseshell glasses perched on the tip of her nose.

"Because free-fall bombs don't need to have any space

devoted to steering fins or other target devices, they can carry a bigger payload than smart bombs. I know there's been some debate, though, about the percent increase in damage. Can you speak to the discrepancy in the schools of thought?" Catherine pushed her glasses farther up on her nose and tapped her pen against her desk impatiently.

Baxter cleared his throat. "You're correct," he said. "Free-fall bombs do carry a bigger payload. The question of the percentage of increase in damage is a tricky one, however, mainly because it has to do with the altitude from which the bomb is dropped. A higher altitude will result in a wider horizontal radius of damage." Catherine furrowed her brows and increased the tempo of her pen tap. "So you're saying the blast impact wouldn't be affected *unless* you were dealing with a bomb dropped from midair?"

"Exactly." Baxter folded his arms across his sturdy chest, looking impressed.

Like Kevin's bomb, Gaia thought again dully. *Kevin's was stationary. So it didn't matter whether or not it had steering fins or a target device. It would have blown us all away regardless.*

It wasn't a comforting thought.

Gaia was also surprised to hear how much Catherine seemed to know about bombs. She had thought that Catherine was a computer-geek programmer, an engineering über-genius. But this extensive knowledge of the anatomy of a bomb? Mildly disturbing.

Or was Gaia the one with the problem? After all, they were being taught this information; clearly it was material that someone deemed them responsible enough to handle. Maybe Catherine was just, in this capacity, a better agent than Gaia. And once again Gaia was letting her past life get the best of her, letting her suspicions run amok. Yes, her uncle had been a terrorist, but she couldn't afford to dwell on that, to let that experience cloud her judgment now. Rather than be surprised by Catherine, Gaia knew, she should be *emulating* her.

"And now the moment I'm sure you've all been waiting for." Agent Baxter rapped his laser pointer against his palm as another pair of agents emerged from side doors at the front of the auditorium. Each agent wheeled a dolly whose cargo was covered by a thick plastic sheet. It was easy enough to guess what lay underneath the sheets.

Bombs, Gaia thought to herself dizzily. *We're going to have to dismantle fake bombs.*

The NATs began to shift in their seats, craning their heads to have a better look at the dollies. The agents parked themselves on either side of the room and began to distribute the small, mechanical-looking objects, one to each trainee.

Gaia shook her head as her bomb was deposited onto her desk with an unceremonious *thud.* She cocked her head and peered at it inquisitively, not wanting to touch it before they were given the official go-ahead, just in case that was part of the drill. One really never knew in this place. The bomb was small, much smaller than she would have expected, but for the most part it really did look like something out of a Vin Diesel movie: a tiny silver box intercut with tangled colored wires and emblazoned with a flashing digital clock that read *12:00.* To either side of her, trainees were poking and prodding at their bombs gingerly.

Agent Baxter set his laser pointer down and picked up a small device that resembled a video-game joystick of sorts. Gaia recognized it instantly. It looked exactly like the detonator Kevin had used. "You have three minutes to disassemble your bomb," Baxter announced. Then he raised the detonator and clicked, without hesitation, on the bright red panic button at its center.

Instantly Gaia's clock skipped down from *12:00* to *3:00* and proceeded to continue to count backward. It was amazing; she knew that these bombs weren't hooked up to any actual explosives, but her adrenal reaction was the same nonetheless. She wasn't afraid, of course—that would be a genetic impossibility— but her heart rate had certainly increased tenfold. That was good. With it came the general sense of calm and focus that came over her during moments when regular folk would be overtaken by fear.

Based on Baxter's little PowerPoint presentation, the trick here was evidently to undo the right wire. It always seemed to work for Vin Diesel, after all. But which one was it? She glanced at the diagram tacked to the wall. The wires in that drawing were gray and blue. The wires on her bomb were green and yellow. She suspected that this was no coincidence.

2:28.

They were being timed against each other, all of the NATs. She was sure of it. Otherwise they'd have been allowed to work in teams. It was really a shame. On a team, her inability to experience fear would be a real asset. However, on her own, her lack of fear wasn't enough to help her to identify the correct wire. The wires in the diagram were clean and crisp and running in predictable patterns; the wires on her bomb were twisted arteries knotted into thick ropes. *Let's work backward,* she thought, gently running her finger along the place where the yellow wire met the edge of the bomb's smooth metal surface. The machine felt warm to her touch. *Okay, now we're getting somewh—*

"Done!"

Gaia whipped around in her seat, unsurprised to see Catherine hunched over her desk, wires neatly separated from the metal body of the bomb with nearly surgical precision. Had she *chewed* the wires off? Gaia was impressed.

As was Agent Baxter. He quickly referred to his stopwatch. "One minute, three seconds. Not bad, Sanders."

"Thank you, sir," she said modestly.

"Sir, I think I've just about—"

"Taylor. The exercise is finished. You did not come in first, and therefore I am not interested."

Gaia felt the sting of Baxter's words as though they were directed at her personally; she recoiled in her head as Will did, literally, in his seat. She could tell by the set of his jaw that he was not taking this reproach well. His face was flushed pink and his mouth was stretched into a thin, tight line.

"Moore."

At the sound of her name, Gaia whipped around. Agent Baxter was standing directly over her, like some dark angel of scary positive reinforcement. He didn't crack a smile, although he appeared to be commending her.

"Well done," he said, not exactly smiling as such but still managing to convey his approval. "Even though you seemed confused and weren't able to defuse the bomb, you were diligent and stuck to your strategy."

"Thank you, sir," Gaia said. If there was one thing she was

26

starting to understand about Quantico, it was that you took praise where you could get it, because it wasn't bandied about all that freely—which was probably why Will's cheeks were blazing red right now.

"You're all dismissed," Baxter said. "Sanders, I'm going to present the results of this exercise to Bishop and Malloy, along with the recommendation that you spend more time on bomb squad detail. That is, if you're interested."

"Oh, I'm interested, sir, definitely," Catherine enthused, rising from her seat and gathering her books. "Absolutely."

All of the NATs began packing their belongings and preparing to leave the lecture hall. Will, however, grabbed his textbook and notebook and headed for the door in a rush.

Gaia dashed after him. "Will," she called.

He turned just as he reached the doorway.

"Wait up," she said. "I just wanted to—"

"Actually, Gaia, I'm in a hurry," he said, smiling to take the edge off. He continued out the door without waiting for her reply. It was becoming a pattern with him.

Gaia stood rooted to the ground, wondering what she had done to garner the wrath of William Taylor. He was competitive, she got that, but so was she, and up until now their respective need to best each other had mainly egged them both on to challenge themselves. Apparently now they had crossed some invisible, intangible threshold, Will's breaking point. Was it their kiss that had done it? Was Will not capable of being involved with someone who was—and here she had to be grudgingly honest with herself—his equal?

She felt a tug at her sleeve. It was Catherine, nudging her. "You ready?" she asked.

"Yup," Gaia said, snapping back into reality. "Wait, what for?"

Catherine frowned. "We have to go meet the medical examiner, remember?"

Gaia nodded. "Right, Ann's autopsy." They had scheduled it the day before.

She hated to admit it, but a part of her really wanted to go after Will and smooth his ruffled feathers. Which made her nuts, because she knew that she didn't actually have anything to apologize for.

It didn't matter, though, because right now, there were much more important tasks at hand.

Gaia

I've made a decision: I just don't care what Will Taylor thinks.

Not one iota.

Oh, sure, I guess he's attractive. I mean, if you're into that super-athletic, towheaded Southern charm.

And he can be funny. For example, when we're out at night, a long day of training behind us, and he suddenly starts quoting from *Silence of the Lambs*, *A Few Good Men*, or basically any other military movie you can think of to lighten the air. His Jack Nicholson impersonation ("You can't handle the truth!") is uncanny.

He's well read, too. I mean, the minute I introduced myself, he immediately recognized my name: *Gaia*, the earth goddess. And maybe this is something that's taught in school, but the fact is, I have spent the better part of my life repeating my name to people who think it's some sort of chemical solvent.

Still, I just can't bring myself to care what he thinks. Because in addition to the beauty-brawn-brains total package thing that he's got going on, he's also fiercely competitive. And I am not fooled by his sweet-as-molasses demeanor (which has not exactly been in full force as of late). Will Taylor is a boy who is used to coming in first. And unfortunately, here at Quantico, he is surrounded by others who are *also* used to coming in first. Which is problematic by definition because, in most competitions, there can only be one clear-cut winner. With any luck, we will all graduate from this training course. But there's still only room for *one* number one among us.

Will thinks it should be him. And sure, he's got lots going for him (see above re: beauty, brawn, brains). But then, Catherine is a master computer programmer, and Kim is an esteemed psychological profiler.

And me? I've got some skills of my own.

Everyone here is special in some way. For my part, I'm hoping that the program will help me to learn and share and build and grow.

Yes, I'm aware I sound like a deranged Hallmark copywriter. About the FBI being like a home to me and yadda yadda. Considering how often I've been shuffled around, that's saying a lot. I know Agent Malloy has his doubts about me, and they're certainly founded. But I'm going to prove him wrong. I'm going to succeed here. And if that means trouncing Will Taylor in the process—however inadvertently—well, stuff happens. I like him—I think—but I need this.

It's frustrating, though. Here I am, turning over a new leaf, spewing mildly psychotic greeting-card platitudes and embracing positivity—and somehow, I still manage to piss people off. I guess that's typical. Especially since the one person I'm pushing away is the one who matters the most to me.

The one who matters the most to me—wait. Did I really just say that? I'm foggy from lack of sleep and stressing about the double duty and the murder case. No way did I just say that. That would be impossible. Because, like I said, I just don't care what Will Taylor thinks.

Not one bit.

overwhelmingly realistic

The medical examiner for Quantico was, in fact, the medical examiner for all of Prince Edward County, and as such, her office was a ways from the academy. The drive over took a good forty minutes, during which Gaia and Catherine sat blanketed in silence in the backseat of an agency sedan. They were driven by Agent Crane, a laconic African-American in his early thirties. He'd briefly introduced himself before they set out as the agent assigned to oversee them, but he'd made it clear that he didn't intend to step on their toes. As Bishop had told them, this really was their show. It was pretty flattering, actually. And also very stressful.

As they moved farther beyond the outskirts of Quantico, Gaia was struck again by how rural so much of the countryside was. The landscape was spare and flat, patches of muddy grassland giving way to swampy inlets. Houses became increasingly spread apart, smaller, and more decrepit. Did people live here? Obviously they did, though the quality of life was clearly lacking. It was a far cry from the coastal cities Gaia had come to know like the back of her hand: New York with its flashing lights, multiethnic blur, and endless, frenetic activity, and San Francisco, a relaxed, open community with a warm vibe and an appreciation for all things outdoors.

But a far cry was just about perfect, Gaia decided. A far cry was exactly what she needed. A fresh start. A chance to reinvent herself. She'd been granted one do-over when she left New York for college, and now, at last, she'd recognized her calling. This wasn't so much a do-over as a do-one-*better*. And so yes, for this endeavor, someplace unknown would do just fine.

Unfortunately, it was all too easy to see that this fresh start had little to do with sunshine and roses. After all, she and Catherine were investigating a murder. A real murder. Gaia could reinvent herself as many times over as she wanted, but Ann? Ann wasn't going to have any more second chances. Which meant that Gaia had to take her new life, her new role, seriously. She couldn't bring Ann back from the dead, but at least she could try to make some sense out of what had happened and bring the killer to justice. It wasn't a wholly comforting thought, but it was something.

"It's a lot farther than Hogan's Alley, huh?" Catherine asked, breaking into Gaia's thoughts.

"Mmm," Gaia said. It was a thought she'd had herself, one that had been floating in the back of her consciousness for the past twenty minutes. She hadn't really wanted to allow it to fully surface. The Hogan's Alley medical examiner, of course, was in the Hogan's Alley complex, right in Quantico, within walking distance of their dorms, the dining hall, and the classroom complexes. It was meticulously rendered and overwhelmingly realistic, but it wasn't real. It was a game. An elaborately staged, high-stakes game. But this? This drive along the Virginia coastline, this not-so-scenic route? It was the route to the real medical examiner's office. Where they would be witnessing a real autopsy.

Catherine made a face. "I'm nervous," she confessed, taking a deep breath and letting it out slowly. "I'm afraid I'm going to freak out or faint or something. I mean, this is the real deal. Aren't you scared?" She gnawed on one fingernail and stared at Gaia wide-eyed, frankly curious.

Gaia paused for a moment, considering. *If only you knew.*

Seeing Ann's corpse at the scene of the crime had been difficult, and she certainly wasn't looking forward to the visit to the medical examiner. She knew it would be terribly painful, even though it was a necessary step toward catching the bastard who'd murdered Ann. So she was on edge, yes. Concerned, definitely.

But afraid? Never.

"I, uh, I guess I'm just not sure what to expect," she said, hoping that her vague answer was appropriate. She checked her watch; they had plenty of time before they were expected at the ME's office and Agent Crane was driving like a reject from the Indy 500, so at least punctuality was one thing they wouldn't have to worry about. She sighed and settled back against her seat, mentally screwing up her . . . well, not her courage, exactly. But her focus. Focus and determination.

They'd be there soon, and Gaia wanted to be ready.

SUDDEN SHIFT IN CLIMATE

Alice Potter was a petite, wiry redhead with sparkling green eyes and a seemingly bottomless reserve of energy. The medical examiner met Gaia, Catherine, and Agent Crane at the front door of her somewhat modest facility with a vigorous stride and a slightly apologetic grin. "I'm afraid we're not a very grand-scale operation," she said, pushing open the double doors and stepping back to allow them inside. She reached out and offered them each a firm handshake. "But our equipment is state-of-the-art and we get the job done."

"That's what we've heard," Gaia said, warming to the woman's upfront sincerity.

"Come on in and I'll give you the grand tour," Alice said, waving them along.

She ushered them down a hallway, their shoes clacking against the scuffed tiled floor in unison. "As you can probably tell, we have two levels here," she said. "This floor and a basement level below. Up here is our library; you can find just about any journal or other literature on forensics, anatomy, and medicine in there. I don't mind telling you that because we're the sole medical-examining facility for the county, we've got a very thorough collection. We have five computer terminals—which, I should mention, are also at your disposal. Your FBI security code should allow you to access their databases, and the computers are automatically linked to our most high-traffic forensic and medical sites."

Gaia peered into the library briefly as they walked past. It looked no bigger than her high school library had been, but a cursory glance at the shelves indicated a vast collection of resource materials, as Alice had just explained. She felt reassured that if they weren't able to track Ann's killer, it wouldn't be due to a lack of information at hand. But not tracking the killer was not an option.

"And this," Alice said, pushing open a glass door to reveal a stark white room lined with white Formica cabinets and two long, steel-topped tables, "is our lab. We have staff who come in when we need to run sample analyses, and we can also send some of our less time-sensitive materials out to larger facilities. But all in all, we prefer to perform the majority of our testing on-site so that we can retain control of the integrity of the lab work."

"That makes sense," Catherine said, her eyes darting across every surface of the space. Gaia could see that Catherine was having the same reaction to Alice's empire that she was; it wasn't overwhelming, but it would definitely be a great place for hands-on experience.

"What's downstairs?" Gaia asked.

"You're one step ahead of me," Alice said, moving swiftly down the hallway to a bright red door marked STAIRS. "That's really where the bulk of my work takes place. Downstairs we have a storage space for the bodies that come in—much like an interim morgue. We call it the cold room, for obvious reasons. And then there's the place where, on any given day, you're most likely to find me: my examining room." She bounded down the steps briskly, taking them two at a time.

They made their way down to the basement level. Gaia immediately noticed a drop in temperature. The entire floor was one big cold room, she thought. But then, that made sense, considering what went on down here. She shivered, and not just at the sudden shift in climate.

Alice came to a halt in front of another ominous set of steel double doors. "Here we are," she said brightly, as though they'd just arrived at a water park or fabulous new hotel—somewhere hip and cool that they were just dying to see from the inside out. All at once, though, her eyes glimmered with somber intent.

"Am I right in assuming that this is the first 'bagged and tagged' corpse that you've witnessed?"

Both girls nodded, heads bobbing up and down in unison.

"I should warn you that your first can be difficult. It's hard to see a body up close, to have to study it intently. I know you've had experience with role-playing at Hogan's Alley. Don't be surprised if this hits you harder than that."

With a grim set to her mouth, Alice pushed open the door.

The first thing that hit Gaia was the smell. It didn't smell . . . well, it didn't smell *bad*, particularly. But it also didn't smell the way she would have expected it to—the room was smothered in the thick, sharp, cloying chemical aroma of a complex formaldehyde cocktail. It was staggering, but it was probably better than any other alternative.

The second thing Gaia noticed was the body.

She'd seen dead bodies before. In fact, she'd seen all too many. She'd seen her high school friend, Mary Moss, shot by Gaia's own twisted uncle, and she'd seen her evil-but-ultimately-redeemed foster mother shot by an assassin she had actually hired to kill Gaia. She had seen her boyfriend Jake ripped apart by bullets right before her eyes and had held him as the life drained from his body. And then there was the door prize, bonus round, final jeopardy of all the corpses that Gaia had known in her (frighteningly short, when you thought about it in this context) day: her mother's. There was no memory Gaia had known that could compare to the vision of her mother's life seeping out from her in the form of puddles, rivers, impossible amounts of blood across the kitchen floor of their Berkshires cottage.

And somehow this was different. Inexplicably, indescribably different.

Seeing Ann's blue-tinged body splayed prone across a sleek slab of steel didn't provoke the intense emotional reaction—like shards of glass to the stomach—in Gaia that Jake's death had. She didn't think that *any* death would hit her the way that Jake's had, the way her mother's had. But this . . . Jake's bullet holes, her mother's lifeless stare—those had been the images of children's picture books compared to this. Whoever had murdered Ann had slit her throat so forcefully that he had nearly decapitated her. And now Gaia was standing some three feet from the ragged, hollow wound.

She swallowed hard and willed the wave of nausea to pass.

"Happens to all of us the first time. It still happens to me."

Gaia steadied her nerves and looked up to see a small man with curly brown hair and a Charlie Chaplin mustache smiling at her with kind eyes.

"Ladies, allow me to introduce my indefatigable assistant," Alice said, clapping the man on the back affably. "Catherine Sanders, Gaia Moore, this is Ben Baker."

Gaia and Catherine both shuffled forward to take turns shaking Ben's proffered hand. "Hey, great to meet you both," he said cheerily, his upbeat persona clashing drastically with the tone of his surrounding environs.

He probably has *to stay upbeat,* Gaia decided. *Or else go completely crazy. All he does, day in and day out, is examine people's corpses. That has to wear on you.*

"So, have there been any interesting developments?" she asked, trying to sound more authoritative than she felt. She took a deep breath through her mouth and stepped closer to the table, even going so far as to lean forward to better examine Ann's neck. She shuddered. The skin around the wound was gray and frayed, as though it had been torn open with a serrated blade. *Which maybe it was,* she thought, feeling sick again. She willed her stomach to unclench.

"We just finished recording all of our notes," Ben said. "You can look at the file if you'd like. It's over on the table by the front door."

"Thanks. We just want to observe her on our own for a minute," Gaia said, folding her arms across her chest and pacing slowly around the table so as to better take in the body in its entirety.

Catherine stood at the far end of the table, near Ann's head. "Cause of death, stab wounds to the throat. Evidence of the killer's intensity," she observed. "Means it's probably a onetime deal rather than the work of a serial killer."

Alice nodded thoughtfully. "Good thinking. A passionate or emotion-driven crime usually suggests that it's personal."

Whoever did this to Ann knew *her,* Gaia thought dully. *The sick bastard was probably someone she considered a friend.*

Her stomach roiling with disgust, she leaned forward. Angry blue bruises stood out like tattoos against the surface of Ann's waxy, pallid skin. Gaia realized that they fell in perfect reverse semicircles. *This means something,* she thought suddenly. *I know this.*

"The, uh, pattern of bruises," she began, her voice sounding too loud in her own head. "They indicate that the killer grabbed her from behind."

"Exactly," Ben said, handing Gaia the file they'd begun. "And the incision across her throat is deep. It wasn't made with an ordinary kitchen knife. My guess is that it was a hunting knife. Something made to go through bone."

Gaia rubbed her hands over her arms, knowing that the sudden chill tiptoeing across her spine had absolutely nothing to do with room temperature.

Alice stepped up to the body. She had snapped a pair of rubber gloves onto her hands, and now she was pointing one latex-covered finger at Ann's neck. "Do you see how the wound is wider here, on the right side of the neck? And then it trails off? That wide section, that's the point of initial penetration, where he stabbed the knife in before dragging it across her neck."

"Meaning the killer is probably left-handed," Gaia said, thinking out loud. She quickly crossed to where Catherine stood and lined herself up behind Catherine, walking herself through the killer's steps. "First he comes up behind her," she said, "and grabs her. That's where the bruises are. Then he pulls out his knife with his left hand—he's probably got his right pinning her arms to her sides—and stabs like this—" She made a swift sweeping motion across Catherine's neck with her closed fist. "Then he hears us, drops her on the ground, and runs."

"But not before you catch a look at him," Catherine said.

Gaia sighed. "Barely. That's the thing—I saw him for a minute, seriously. Not even. Thirty seconds. Not to mention, he was wearing a ski mask."

"Not a lot to go on," Catherine admitted. "But people have solved crimes with less."

Gaia held out her hand, ticking off the facts. "Well, okay. What do we know? The killer is left-handed and either hunts or shops at sporting or hunting stores. He apparently knew—and hated—Ann." Her shoulders slumped. "It's nothing. It's not enough." She shrugged, feeling helpless.

"So what now?" Catherine asked.

"First, you'll have to read our report and sign off on our findings. Then you follow up on any leads," Alice said. "I'm sure that if you go over the facts again, another detail will present itself. It always does."

"Why don't we send Ann's clothing to the lab for a fiber analysis?" Gaia suggested. "I mean, there's a good chance that nothing will turn up, but it's worth asking, don't you think?"

"Yes," Alice said, smiling encouragingly. "Yes, I do."

FEDERAL BUREAU OF INVESTIGATION
FIELD REPORT—QUANTICO SPECIAL FORCES TRAINING PROGRAM

REPORT: <u>Case #261</u>

SUPERVISORS: <u>Special Agent Hyde, Special Agent Crane, codes B76 and B34</u>

SUMMARY: Temporary Agents Moore and Sanders arrived at the Prince Edward County Morgue at 14:00 hours, where they were met by ME Alice Potter and her assistant, Benjamin Baker. Potter and Baker walked the agents through the facilities and then directed them to the victim's body. Body had already been autopsied, but agents examined the body for physical evidence (see attached file detailing findings). Follow-up to include lab analysis of victim's clothing.

"Handwriting analysis?" Catherine grumbled, pushing her short dark hair out of her eyes impatiently. "What is this, a kiddie birthday party?" She stared at the blank sheet of paper in front of her with murderous intent. "There are more important places for us to be, Gaia," she said.

"I know," Gaia agreed. Scribbling some lines out for some weird pseudo-shrink to scrutinize did feel pretty hokey, especially after the morning they'd had with the medical examiner. It was really difficult to come back to Quantico and plug right back into their regular responsibilities. Every time Gaia blinked, the image of Ann's gaping wound flashed across the inside of her eyelids. "But we promised we would be able to balance training with the case, and I think that means . . ." She trailed off, gesturing limply at the room full of NATs, grouped in clusters at individual tables, each regarding his blank sheet of paper with measured skepticism.

"True, handwriting analysis is considered a pretty soft means of profiling," Kim said, cutting in, "but it can be a helpful supplement to a case. When you're dealing with an unbalanced criminal, every little piece of information you can possibly gather really helps." He didn't look annoyed or suspicious, like everyone else. He looked downright eager. He'd been clutching his mechanical pencil to his chest like a trophy ever since they'd sat down.

"*You* look pretty okay about being here," Gaia said, looking at Will. It was true: he was dressed casually, in faded jeans and a stretched-out T-shirt, and though he didn't look nearly as thrilled to write out his name on his paper as Kim did, he didn't look impatient either. "Do you believe in this stuff?"

Will smiled. "Well, I sure wouldn't take a handwriting analysis the end-all word on someone's personality, but I can't see how it could hurt to play along," he said, the long consonants rolling off his tongue softly.

Agent Malloy stood at the front of the room. His thick hair was shellacked back with gel and his skin was tight and shiny. It looked to Gaia like he hadn't slept in days, but then, she supposed he always looked that way. Hard. Tense. He didn't look like he thought handwriting analysis was particularly hokey. Which definitely meant that the rest of them would have to take it seriously, too.

"You should all have read the section on handwriting analysis in your books last night," Malloy said gruffly, referring to a bound collection of relevant secondary sources that the FBI provided for all of its trainees. "I'd like for you each to write out, as naturally as possible, the sentence 'The quick brown fox jumps over the lazy dog.' We'll take one volunteer to offer his or her work up to the classroom, and then you will break up into individual groups and look over each other's work and offer opinions. I should stress," he added, anticipating the students' next question, "that there really are no right answers. Handwriting analysis isn't a science, and therefore it can only offer certain clues when used in profiling. It should never be used as a definitive study of a character, or on its own."

The room fell silent as the students awaited further instructions from Malloy. He looked puzzled. "Are you writing?" he asked, prompting them. The students immediately began to do so.

Gaia leaned forward and scratched out the sentence quickly, unselfconsciously. She looked around her table. Catherine was gripping her pencil tightly, taking deliberate strokes. Kim must have finished already; he was leaning back in his chair with his hands folded calmly in his lap.

Will's pencil dipped in graceful flourishes across the page. After a moment he put it back down and tilted his seat back, grinning smugly.

"I trust you're all finished?" Malloy asked after a few moments, breaking into the slightly awkward silence that had fallen over the room. "May I have a volunteer? Tate?" he prompted, nodding at a short, slight Irish girl with straight, shoulder-length light brown hair and nervous hazel-hued eyes who was camped out in the front row and probably cursing herself for it. Reluctantly Tate leaned forward in her seat, stretching out her arm to pass the paper to Malloy.

He plucked it from her and put it under a projector. "Any thoughts?" he asked, throwing the question out to no one in particular.

People shifted in their seats, but no one offered up an opinion.

Malloy cleared his throat. "Do I take this to mean that none of you have done the reading?" he asked, sounding displeased.

"Her *t*'s," Kim said, pointing. "They're crossed predominantly on the left side."

"Signifying?"

"A tendency to procrastinate," Kim said mildly, somehow managing to make it sound like less of an insult. "Also, she's taken some harsh strokes at the beginning of her words, which could indicate resentment."

"Good, good," Malloy said, nodding. "What else?"

"The, uh, the loops at the ends of her letters—those are a sign of a desire for attention," someone in the back row called out. "Like a little kid raising his hand."

Tate's face had morphed from an expression of vague annoyance to a thundercloud threatening to erupt. Her reaction did not go unnoticed by Gaia.

"The strokes on her *n* and *m* are needle sharp," Gaia chimed in. "Which means she's probably a quick thinker."

Tate flashed Gaia a grateful smile.

"Also true," Malloy agreed. He clapped. "Well, it looks like I was wrong and at least some of you *have* done the reading"— he glanced meaningfully at both Kim and Gaia as he said this—"which bodes well. This isn't a drill since, as I said, it's really a matter of educated opinion. But I'd like you to spend some time discussing the samples you've created at your table. At the end of class, please pass your samples along with your group's comments to me."

"Tate looks pretty pissed," Catherine observed as she, Gaia, Will, and Kim turned back to their group. "That's my educated opinion."

"Well, she wants attention," Gaia pointed out. "Or so her handwriting indicated. I think we're all going to need to have pretty thick skin around here."

"I think you're right," Kim said. He reached across the table and snatched up Catherine's sample. "Starting with you, dearie." He winked.

She stuck her tongue out at him teasingly. "Go ahead—I have nothing to hide."

Nothing to hide, Gaia thought, suddenly seized by a cold feeling of dread. She didn't have anything to *hide* per se, but this whole having friends, trusting people thing was still pretty new to her. She wasn't sure she was ready to give them a hand-engraved portal into her psyche. Even a "soft" portal.

Will regarded Catherine's sample pensively. "For starters, look at her *s* in *Sanders*," he said, sitting up straight in his seat. "It's twice the size of her other letters, even though it's at the end of a word. That's defiance."

"Right, good," Kim said, struggling to write quickly enough to keep up with what Will was saying.

"I'm a rebel," Catherine quipped.

"Your *r*'s and your *h*'s are very square," Gaia pointed out. "Manual dexterity. I guess you probably need that for the computer programming and stuff."

"What about you, Kim?" Catherine asked suddenly, shifting herself out of the limelight. "I don't see you volunteering your page up for analysis."

"It's all yours," he said, entirely unperturbed.

She held his sheet up in front of her, clearly looking for issues. After a moment of scanning, her face fell. She peered up at him. "You're pretty normal," she said.

"I prefer the term *well adjusted*," Kim corrected.

"Your *o*'s are wide and round—that's frankness, openness, and generosity," Gaia said, leaning over Catherine's shoulder for a better look.

"Saint Kim, I do declare, I'm very impressed," Will joked, over-enunciating his drawl until he sounded like a refugee from a summer-stock production of *The Long, Hot Summer.*

"What have *you* got for us, Dixie?" Catherine asked. She slid Will's sheet across the table to Kim. "Check it out."

"Well, the loops at the tops of your capital letters indicate a clear-cut desire for responsibility," Kim said. "No surprise, considering you were in line for the Olympics before the pesky FBI got in your way."

"Yes, but the downward slant to your *t* bar says *domineering*," Catherine interjected. "Responsibility, sure, but you want to be the queen bee."

Was it Gaia's imagination, or did a hint of annoyance flicker across Will's face? She suppressed a grin. It was true: Will wanted responsibility *and* he wanted to be on top. That could have ramifications for their relationship—if they ever managed to sort their feelings out.

"It's slanted, and it's also sharp," Kim said. "Could be that you have two temperaments. The sharp, slashing motions imply that you can be difficult when you don't get your way. That's when your dark side emerges. But of course, when things are going well, it's as though you're an entirely different person."

"Fortunately, I always get my way," Will said smoothly, winking.

Well, what about when you lose to your fellow classmates? Gaia thought, remembering the first day of training, when Will had come in second to her during an obstacle course race. At the time, he had played the Southern gentleman for all he was worth, but Gaia knew that he'd been gnashing his teeth in frustration the entire time.

"I want to see what's on Gaia's mind," Will said abruptly.

Go ahead, Gaia thought. *I'm not afraid.*

Kim scrunched down in his seat, his forehead wrinkled in concentration. "Yours is good, Gaia," he said, grinning eagerly.

"Glad to be a source of entertainment," Gaia said, half kidding.

He gestured toward her sample. "Check out the breakaway *p* with the high upstroke. You're attentive to detail and an analytical thinker."

Gaia mimed patting herself on the back.

"True, but now—and you can correct me if I'm wrong—I do believe that sort of *p* also indicates aggressive tendencies," Will said, smirking at Gaia.

Touché, she thought. *I'm working on it.*

"And look—" he said, gesturing. "The lower loops of your *y* and *j* are retraced completely. Antisocial behavior. Inability to trust."

Gaia opened her mouth to respond, then closed it promptly. Fortunately, at that moment, Malloy strode back to the front of the room. "Time's up, people. I'm sure there's somewhere else you're supposed to be. Please pass your group's work up to me on your way out the door."

Kim hastily scrawled the last few notes they'd discussed on the bottom of Gaia's sample. "I'm never going to be able to handwrite something for the FBI again without being completely paranoid," he said, not entirely joking.

"I'm sure they don't care, Kim," Catherine said.

I'm not, Gaia thought.

She wasn't sure of that at all. This was the organization, after all, that had kept a file on her for at least the past three years, if not longer. There was no reason to assume that they weren't going to add this to her dossier.

She couldn't decide how she felt about that fact, either. She was slightly stunned to discover that her handwriting sample actually revealed some truth about her personality. In particular, the truths she'd gone to great lengths to reinvent. She didn't want to be the angry vigilante adolescent, picking fights with random scuzzballs in Washington Square Park. She wanted to be Gaia Moore, keen FBI trainee and cool, easygoing roommate. She wanted to be fun, smart, talented. Capable of getting along with other people. Normal.

But apparently the information revealed by the smallest sample of her handwriting suggested that she wasn't quite there yet.

Discouraging.

She peered discreetly at her friends. Kim didn't seem fazed at all by the exercise. Of course, his handwriting hadn't revealed anything shady at all. Catherine, on the other hand, was evidently adept but possibly rebellious. What could that mean?

And then there was Will.

Competitive, achievist Will. Apparently he was driven, ambitious, and a sore loser. She'd hardly needed a handwriting sample to figure that out. She hadn't known for certain, of course, when she met him that he'd be the type to pitch a grand temper tantrum when his butt was beaten by a girly-girl, but it hadn't taken all that long to put two and two together. His very being was the embodiment of duality: a smooth-as-honey, mannered peach with a hard-as-tire-irons thirst for success.

She shouldered her messenger bag—some things never went out of style—and headed for the door after Kim and Catherine. She paused briefly. Will would know to follow, right? He didn't need a formal invitation to go to lunch, did he? She turned around to see him methodically gathering his books in a neat stack before tucking them under his arm. His face was pulled taut in an impatient grimace, but the expression dissolved when he felt Gaia's gaze on him. He looked up.

"Waiting for me?" he asked pleasantly. "That's awfully *social.*"

For the second time in less than ten minutes, Gaia again found herself at a loss for words. She stood stock-still in place, gaping at Will.

He came up beside her and linked his arm through hers. "Let's go then, shall we, darling?" he asked. And without further ado, he led her off to lunch.

If she was going to get to the bottom of what was going on between them, it wasn't going to happen this afternoon.

Will

Responsible, that's me. I've been responsible Will Taylor since the day I was born. I was the oldest, which carried with it its own set of expectations, and then, as it turned out, I was the only child. I thought I was my parents' sun, moon, and stars.

But it turned out I thought wrong.

It turned out I had to *work* for affection, for respect, for love. And so I did. I was the model child: chores, errands, homework, you name it, I did it. Anything my mother asked of me, anything that would have made her life easier once . . .

Well, anything.

It turned out, I was pretty good at the book learnin', which was convenient. But I wasn't socially maladjusted, either. One day, on my way home from school, an older kid—Thompson McCullen—challenged me to a race. He was older and bigger, and he cheated. Jumped out in front of me a split second before the countdown ended. But I ran faster than I'd ever known I could, mainly because I was so angry, and I beat him. By a decent amount, too. The soles of my feet were practically smoking, but I knew I'd stumbled onto something. If I close my eyes, I can still see Thompson, standing at the corner of my mom's street, fists clenched at his sides, scruffy hair damp with sweat, scowling.

I remember thinking, *Sore loser.*

Now I understand what he was feeling that day. What it must have been like to lose to someone younger, someone half his size. In the same way that beating him gave me a newfound sense of pride, losing to me must have had the reverse effect on him. He'd probably spent his entire preadolescent life, up until that moment, believing a certain thing about himself, only to have the rug yanked out from under him by a snotty little kid. And he must have doubted himself.

The same way I doubt myself around Gaia.

It kills me, this feeling. Would you believe, I was actually *nervous* during the handwriting analysis? I was worried that Kim would take one look at my sample and pronounce his diagnosis: *jealousy*. Because that's what it is, plain and simple. I'm jealous.

I wish that I weren't. There's a part of me that's drawn to Gaia so intensely that I can barely breathe when I'm near her, and that part of me wishes I could put aside my need to prevail. I don't want to dominate her. I want to . . . well, I'm not sure. I still haven't been able to figure that part out. Because every time I get within ten feet of her, something in my system short-circuits, and suddenly all I can think about, all I can feel, is her electric presence, humming next to mine. But she's not stupid. Far from it. She may be one of the first people I've ever met who's able to keep up with me. And she can tell. She can tell that Kim's right, that these days I'm acting like a spoiled child whose life has been turned upside down by the arrival of a baby sister. Someone who's shoving me out of the limelight—even if it's wholly unintentional.

My anger, my envy, my insert-your-own-armchair-analysis-HERE is getting in the way. Not just between myself and Gaia, but among the others as well. Catherine and Kim—*especially* Kim—they can see it, feel it. And it's sending everyone's dynamic two steps to the left. Not enough to throw us completely off, mind you. But enough that we're all moving one count behind the beat. And none of us can afford that. After all, we came here to win. We came here because we are people accustomed to getting what we want. And we're *going* to come out on top.

Well, at least I am.

pale scrubs and
soft-soled shoes

The next day Catherine was woken by Gaia even before breakfast. Her roommate wanted to hit the lab to get the results on the fiber analysis they'd sent in on Ann's clothing. Sleep-fuzzy, Catherine blearily pointed out that the lab wouldn't be open for at least another hour. And that technically, they could just as easily call. It took some convincing, but finally Gaia allowed herself to be dissuaded, taking off for a run to burn some energy before it was time to leave for real. But not before insisting that they visit the lab *in person*. Her theory was that it was crucial that they befriend the technicians who worked there. Catherine could hardly argue—especially not at that hour. Thankfully, after Gaia had gone off jogging, Catherine had somehow managed to drift back off for another half an hour.

The hardest adjustment to life at Quantico, she had found, was the schedule. To say that she was at heart a night owl was an understatement. Typically, she couldn't function before noon. In college she had arranged her classes accordingly, generally spending the wee hours of the night crouched over her PowerBook, the glow of the computer screen a hypnotic beacon spurring her on and drawing her into her work. It didn't matter how late she stayed up, tapping away furiously at her keyboard. She could always make up for it in the morning.

Not so at Quantico, where precious sleep was hard to come by, yet direly needed for performance. Catherine had always been athletic and fit, but never had she tested the limits of her endurance as she was being asked to now. Before, a five-mile run had been what she considered a solid workout. Here it was a warm-up.

She was a generally self-satisfied person, but as she and Gaia strode across the campus to the lab, Catherine found herself envying the tall, lithe blond briefly. Gaia's physical prowess was intimidating. The girl was tall and slender, all sinew and smooth, carved muscle. She outpaced the rest of the NATs on every training run—even Will, and he'd been an Olympic contender.

But it was obvious that Gaia's athleticism was something that came naturally to her, something she was good at almost without thinking. And, it wasn't her only talent. Far from it.

Yes, it was a good thing Catherine's self-esteem was firmly in place. Otherwise a friendship with Gaia Moore would have been a threatening prospect indeed.

"Slow down, Speed Racer," she called, scrambling for a step or two to keep pace with Gaia. "My legs are shorter than yours."

Gaia paused. "Sorry," she said. "I just really want to get there."

"No kidding," Catherine said. "I can feel the stress coming off you in waves. It's like radiation." She could, too. Gaia was desperate to put Ann's killer away—that much was obvious. Catherine was glad they were on the same page. That was something, at least. She knew they had a long, probably grueling investigation process ahead of them. It would help if they agreed about their approach.

Gaia exhaled loudly. "Zen was never my thing," she admitted.

They walked in silence across the grassy expanse of the campus, Catherine enjoying the crisp August scent that signified the slight cooling of summer. She loved seasons, particularly transitional months. Fall, spring . . . she preferred them to the extreme climates of winter and summer. Shades of gray were always more interesting to her.

"This is it," Catherine said, jerking her head toward an imposing industrial-looking building. "I saw it when I came down here for my interview."

They walked inside. The lab was clean, sterile, and antiseptic. The girls moved silently across gleaming white-tiled floors. "Any idea where the fiber analysis lab is?" Catherine wondered aloud.

Gaia had stopped before a floor plan. "We're here," she said, pointing to a large red dot that indicated the front entrance. "It looks like it's just down the hall on the left. Room one-oh-six." She bounced on the balls of her feet once for good measure and took off in that direction.

Walking into room 106 was like walking onto the set of a contemporary science-fiction movie. Every visible surface shone clean and spotless. White tile, Formica, and stainless steel prevailed. Sleek iBooks whirred away on translucent desktops, and lab workers scuttled silently across the floor in pale scrubs and soft-soled shoes.

"Can I help you?"

A tall, thin man of Southeast Asian descent stepped forward, looming in front of Gaia and Catherine. His voice was so unexpectedly deep that Catherine nearly jumped.

She gathered her composure. "Yes, I'm Agent Sanders, and this is Agent Moore."

Recognition flashed across his face. "Of course. You sent in the clothing from the morgue yesterday. I'm Henry. I'm an analyst here. You're in luck: we've just run it through the scanner."

"Scanner?" Gaia asked. "Can you show us how it works?"

"Of course." He ushered them to a large machine resting kitty-corner against the far wall.

At first glance, to Catherine it resembled a CAT-scan machine. She'd had to have a CAT scan when she was much, much younger and experiencing chronic migraines. Her eleven-year-old self had found the whole experience to be "really cool!" The migraines had disappeared around the same time she'd discovered computers.

"You run them through this?" she asked. "And it takes x-rays?"

He nodded. "Exactly. Any trace fiber or oils left behind by the perp, this machine'll find them."

"And what has it found on Ann's clothing?" Gaia asked brusquely.

Gaia's all business, Catherine thought. She couldn't decide how she felt about that. Gaia was productive, of course, which made her a great partner . . . but she was also pretty hard-core. Catherine was feeling rattled, but she tried not to let it show.

Henry shook his head tightly. "Not much, I'm afraid. We got some strands that look like they came from a sweater, but the chemical pattern suggests a pretty standard wool fabric."

"Wool, like army-navy?" Gaia guessed. "Like a fisherman's sweater?"

It would be consistent with the hunting knife as murder weapon, Catherine mused. *A sportsman, using the tools and accessories that he's most familiar with, or at least ones he'd see where he shops.*

"Yes," Henry concurred. "And gloves. Like a fisherman would wear during cold weather. But nothing unique. I mean, you can find sweaters and gloves like this anywhere."

Gaia swore under her breath. "Right. We don't even know that this guy actually fishes."

Catherine felt like swearing herself. "This is Virginia, for Christ's sake," she mumbled. "It's a fishing community. How the hell are we supposed to find the one who killed Catherine?"

Henry offered her a small smile. "Honestly?" he asked, pushing his glasses farther up onto his nose. "I'm just not sure."

MINOR SET-BACKS

The more they worked on Ann's case together, the more Catherine found herself impressed with Gaia's strength and composure. When Henry had informed them that there was simply no way to further narrow down the fiber analysis of Ann's clothes, Catherine had wanted to throw herself onto her bed kicking and screaming. *This,* this dead-end, counterproductive, endlessly frustrating result was the reason she preferred computers to people. Computers were reliable. All you had to do was know how to talk to them. Enter in a code, a program, and set the computer to run that program. Simple. As long as you knew the language, you knew that it was going to work just fine.

Gaia, to the best of Catherine's knowledge, had nothing more than a layperson's familiarity with computers—provided that layperson was a genius of sorts. But it was clear the girl had little patience for minor set-backs. Nonetheless, Gaia had remained cool, calm, and levelheaded throughout the morning at the lab. And when she'd learned that they were stymied, she had turned to Catherine and calmly suggested that they head back to the site of the murder—Ann's house.

"Sure," Catherine had said. "Any particular reason?"

"Well, yeah," Gaia said, managing to sound simultaneously deflated and determined. "We've got nothing left to go on. The only thing I can think of is to head back to the scene and scour the area for new leads. There *must* be something we're missing."

"Let's hope so," Catherine said.

The crime scene, however, was far from inspiring. Less than a week had passed since the crime, and yellow police tape still flashed angrily on every available surface. Catherine and Gaia had to gingerly tiptoe over the ropes and other blockades so as not to disturb anything. Agent Crane surveyed the scene, jotting down observations in a notebook.

Inside, the sense of suspended time, of a stillness consisting of frozen activity, was palpable. In every corner, signs of thwarted life blared at them: a half-eaten bowl of cereal sitting on the kitchen table, soggy, waterlogged *o*'s of some variety floating list-lessly amid curdling milk; an overturned toy truck lyinng on the living room floor; a stack of opened envelopes sitting on a hall table. Ann had been killed during the course of a regular day, one filled with chores, parenting, bills, errands. Here her entire life waited for her, as though at any moment she'd walk through the front door and step right back into her old life, so brutally snatched from her.

It was the truck that bothered Catherine the most. Seeing it reminded her that Ann's son, Sam, was now without a father *or* a mother. He was in court custody, since where he'd end up permanently was still under debate. She had reached down to pick up the truck and move it somewhere, maybe take it to Sam's bedroom so that it didn't look so forlorn on the floor away from all the rest of his toys, when she realized: she couldn't disrupt the crime scene.

That was just it: this was a crime scene. It *wasn't* just frozen stillness. Every dish in the kitchen sink, each pencil discarded on a countertop represented a fragment of Ann's life to which she would never return.

"Did you find anything?" she called up the stairs to Gaia, who'd decided to give Ann's closet another once-over.

"Sure," Gaia said casually, descending the staircase. "Ann wore a size four. And she mostly shopped at that local dress shop. Which isn't all that helpful. Unless the killer worked there." She ran her fingers through her hair, stressed. "God, we are getting nowhere. This is killing me."

"He could have worked there," Catherine said, wanting to be encouraging. "They do carry sweaters. It would make sense. I mean, we really can't rule anything out."

Gaia wasn't looking at her anymore, though. She was staring out beyond Catherine, fixated on a point in the living room. Catherine followed her gaze, realizing what Gaia was looking at.

"Yeah, it's pretty disturbing," she said softly.

She turned so that she too could take in the gruesome sight of the chalk outline of Ann's body on the floor. She had thought it was something that the police only did in books, but there it was, etched onto the floor, an ugly, glaring reminder that a person had laid slain in that very spot, dead at the hands of another human being.

Gaia extended her leg so that she was effectively pointing with her toe. "That's blood."

There was a huge splotch of dried, crusted blood that pooled around the neck of the outlined figure. It conjured up images of Ann lying in that very position, blood gathering thick and dark under her severed neck.

Gaia crept up to the outline and crouched next to it, leaning so far forward, her forehead nearly touched the ground. "What are the chances that this blood is anyone's other than Ann's?"

"Slim to nil," Catherine said simply.

"Yeah, I think you're right," Gaia agreed. She sat down cross-legged on the floor and slid her bag off her shoulder. She reached in and fished out a small plastic pack from which she retrieved a glass slide and a straight edge. She began scraping delicately at the dried blood with the straight edge, depositing the scrapings onto the slide without once touching her finger to them.

Crane returned from his recon in the kitchen and peered over Gaia's shoulder inquisitively. "We already determined that this is Ann's blood," he pointed out.

"True." Gaia sighed. "But I don't have any better ideas. Do you?"

"No," Catherine said sadly. "I don't."

ABO ANTIGEN LEVELS NORMAL

TRACE RHO NEGATIVE

Gel electrophoresis indicates presence of one polymorphism, suggesting that sample is derived from one unique subject.

"We've been talking about profiling and the various means that we have of analyzing a criminal's persona," Agent Bishop said, pacing steadily back and forth across the front of the lecture hall. She wore a crisp navy suit that highlighted her brassy, auburn hair and she took short, clipped strides that were probably a result of the cut of her skirt, which was straight and hit just below her knees. Her green eyes blazed.

"Can anyone tell me about the different character traits of a serial killer versus a single-victim murderer?"

"Serial killers are more detached." It was Tate, who had cautiously planted herself in the back row this afternoon so as to avoid a repeat of her "volunteerism" of the previous morning's handwriting analysis exercise.

"Yes," Bishop said. "Serial killers are true sociopaths. They kill in order to act out their own pathology, with no connection to their victims."

"Their victims symbolize whatever it is that triggers their own neuroses," Kim cut in, warming to the subject. "Issues with their mother, their father, their sexuality. That's why they kill anonymously. They're looking to reenact the same dynamic over and over again rather than to impose violence upon or exact dominance over a particular person. It's more about expressing psychological issues than about hurting an individual person. To them, the person they kill is only an object. And all of their victims fit the same profile."

Gaia sat up in her seat, startled. She'd known Kim was a psych whiz, but his extensive knowledge about the lifestyle and habits of mass murderers was actually slightly creepy. Creepy and mildly fascinating. She raised her hand and began speaking without waiting to be called on. "Either way, it's a crime of passion."

Gaia couldn't help but think about Ann. As of right now, they had to assume her murder was an isolated incident. Meaning that she'd been killed by someone who knew her and knew her well, at that. Someone who'd been pretty obsessed with her for one reason or another. Who was also left-handed and either fished or dressed like someone who did.

But who was that?

AN OVERSIZED HIGH SCHOOL GYM

Here we go again.

It was another cloudless, blue-skied afternoon in Quantico, a gentle breeze playing off the water and blowing into the mainland to offer cool respite from the humidity. By early evening the temperature was supposed to drop and an evening rain shower had been forecast, but for now it was the perfect day to picnic in the grass barefoot, go for a bike ride, or just enjoy a stroll outside.

Whatever. Unfortunately, Gaia wouldn't be tiptoeing through the tulips anytime soon.

She and the other nineteen NATs were in a massive indoor training facility, one that was not unlike an oversized high school gym. They stood atop thick blue mats, lined up in two rows, faced off against each other. Clearly this was some sort of combat drill, but if the NATs were learning anything at all here, it was never to assume that they knew what was coming. They all stood in their FBI-issued workout wear: navy track pants and a navy T-shirt emblazoned with the FBI insignia on the shoulder and the lower hip, respectively. Gaia's shirt was too big on her, but regulations stated that all trainees had to tuck their shirts in during drills, so tuck she did. The edges of the shirt hem were practically grazing her thighs. She aligned her posture and tried to ignore it.

She stared straight ahead, unblinking. How had this happened? She was standing directly across from Will, of all people. Will, who'd been weird to her ever since last Friday night, when he'd gone all dramatic about Gaia and Catherine's temporary badges. Things still hadn't gotten back to normal between them. Come to think of it, things never really *had* been normal between them to begin with. And now they were facing off.

Agent Conroy, a stout but fit man with thick gray hair, stood at the edge of the double line. He regarded the trainees. "People, you will notice that you are lined up in two rows, directly opposite another trainee. No doubt when you picked your position, you paid little mind to the person across from whom you were standing. Which means that the person across from you may or may not be an even match for your strength."

Sparring, Gaia realized. *We're going to be sparring.*

A slow smile spread across Will's face.

And he thinks he can take me.

As Conroy said, when he had ordered the NATS to line up in two columns, he hadn't explained to them why, so most of them had complied without giving too much thought to the person across from them. That had been a mistake, Gaia could see now.

"As field agents, you're going to come across perps of all

shapes and sizes," Conroy continued. "You will need to be able to take down your opponent regardless of these factors. You will need to be prepared to fight anyone, at any time. That is what this drill is for."

"The obstacle courses we've been running have helped you hone your speed, strength, and agility. You haven't been trained in proper sparring because we needed to improve your basic skills first and foremost. This drill is to assess your base level in hand-to-hand, weapons-free combat."

The NATs began to shift in place nervously, rolling shoulders backward and jiggling knees in a last-minute attempt to loosen up. Gaia had no idea how this drill was being measured. She figured that whoever was pinned first would lose. She glanced at Will. The casual smile he usually wore had been replaced by a glint in his eye of pure steel. She cracked her knuckles and rolled back and forth on the balls of her feet.

Agent Conroy raised the whistle he wore around his chest to his lips and blew into it sharply. The shrill sound bounced off the gymnasium walls.

"Go," he said simply.

The trainees to the left and right of Gaia pounced on each other, seduced by the no-holds-barred angle. Of course they had to adhere to the code of conduct as outlined in the field behavior directions, but there was no particular technique they were being asked to utilize. She could hear moans, grunts, and the sounds of scuffling, could feel the impact of bodies slamming against each other.

The smile had returned to Will's face, Gaia could see. More

than a smile. It was a grin, like that of the cat who ate the canary. Or planned to eat it, anyway.

Think again, Tweety.

Just because she had decided to be Little Miss Special Agent Rah Rah Sunny-side Up didn't mean she had to *let* the big, strong macho man win. Gaia had never needed weapons, and she'd never lost a street fight in her life. She wasn't about to start losing now.

Will stepped forward. Gaia stepped forward with her opposite foot. Will struck out with his left arm and Gaia parried with her right. Gaia struck with her left arm; Will parried with his left. Gaia stepped forward and Will stepped back. Will stepped forward and Gaia stepped back. *Step, step, strike, block. Step, step, strike, block.* They were practically dancing, an uncomplicated two-step of measured aggression, a tango that was tinged with the faint flush of . . . their undeniable attraction.

No. No way.

Wham!

At the totally unexpected and *highly* unwelcome thought of her sexual feelings for Will, Gaia's concentration faltered. The lapse lasted only a moment, but that was enough. Will used his momentary advantage to sweep his leg around in a low roundhouse and bring her down. She landed backward on her tailbone, gracelessly.

"Ooh," she said, her breath squeezing out of her diaphragm in an involuntary rush.

"Check," Will said, a smirk plastered across his blindingly white teeth.

Okay, then, Gaia thought. *The gloves are off.*

She rose, taking a split second to dust off the seat of her track pants.

And then she was on him.

In a flash Gaia stretched backward and extended her leg for a high side kick. She was inches from connecting with his shoulder when Will's reflexes kicked in and he grabbed at her ankle. She wobbled briefly, then flexed at her core, bent the leg, hauled backward, and kneed him.

He went down and Gaia was on top of him. She straddled him and he pushed her off, grunting. She rushed forward and pulled him into an elbow lock, but he leaned forward, sending her sprawling over his back and flat onto her own. She landed with a thud and he was on top of her, knees pressed into her chest. He grabbed her wrists and pinned them on either side of her.

Gaia's heart drummed a crazed punk-rock beat against her rib cage. She couldn't shake him. She couldn't. He was splayed atop her with all of his body weight in such a way that she wouldn't be able to muster up enough momentum to throw him off. Had she lost? Her back was slick with sweat that had seeped through her shirt and onto the mat. Will's breathing came in short, staccato breaths.

Suddenly Gaia found herself wondering what it would feel like if he were to lean forward and kiss her right now.

No! Bad thought!

She knew what kissing Will felt like, but now was not the time to let herself get even more distracted.

The sound of the whistle roused her. The drill was over? It had hardly even begun. And . . . she was pinned.

Conroy began weaving through the grand-scale game of Twister he'd created. He talked to each of the pairs, commenting on various aspects of their sparring. But he paused when he got to Gaia and Will.

"Sir," Will said, nodding deferentially.

"You can dismount, Taylor," Conroy said, his voice thick with condescension. "Drill's over."

"Yes, sir," Will said, immediately peeling himself off Gaia and bounding back to a standing "ready" position. Gaia unwound her legs and followed suit.

"You two were an interesting pair to watch," Conroy commented. "Taylor, clearly you were ultimately able to gain the upper hand, as you had Moore pinned when the drill ended. But I must say, Moore, given the discrepancy between your size and Taylor's, you were a highly formidable opponent. You certainly do know how to use your size and your strengths to your advantage. I'm going to have to declare this match a draw."

Yes! Gaia felt like a modern-day Goliath, though she was slightly offended at the suggestion that the match was so incredibly uneven. She nodded at Conroy and turned to face Will. "Congratulations," she said, chucking him on the shoulder like they were old fraternity buddies. All around her, the other NATs were doing the same. "Good match."

Will's smile was gone, though. In fact, Will's expression was curiously devoid of any and all emotion. He'd gone all Agent Pod Person in the time it had taken for Agent Conroy to utter the word *draw*.

Will looked at the spot where Gaia's hand had touched his shoulder. "Yeah," he said shortly. "You did great."

FEDERAL BUREAU OF INVESTIGATION
FIELD REPORT—QUANTICO SPECIAL FORCES TRAINING PROGRAM

REPORT: Hand-to-Hand, Undirected

SUPERVISOR: Special Agent David Conroy, code B49

SUMMARY:

As in previous years, undirected hand-to-hand proceeded according to our expectations: in general, larger, stronger trainees had the advantage. Trainees did engage in "fair fighting" as detailed in our code of conduct. No surprises, with one extreme exception.

While Gaia Moore did, ultimately, find herself overpowered by partner Will Taylor, it should be noted that she sustained the upper hand throughout all but the final moments of the spar, using both the advantages of her build and her keen knowledge and skill. This is consistent with the background information we have on Moore. While she is still to be regarded as a potential loose cannon, Miss Moore is more than ever one to watch.

"Will!" Gaia loped across the green toward Will's retreating figure, wanting to catch him before he disappeared back into his dorm room. *"Will!"*

Goddamn it, Will, slow down so I can talk to you.

He had stormed out immediately after the sparring session, apparently not satisfied with having beaten Gaia in light of the fact that Gaia's technique had been commended. Which was ridiculous. If they both worked at it, with any luck they'd *both* graduate, no? And at the end of the day, wasn't that what they were both after? Graduating number one in the class was a nifty goal, sure, but really, Gaia just wanted that badge. For real.

She broke into a light jog, quickly closing the space between the two of them. She reached out and grabbed at him, catching the edge of his T-shirt between her fingertips. He continued to move forward until the tension snapped him backward lightly.

He stopped short, sighing. He turned to face Gaia. "Yes?" he asked, his face a calm, measured question mark.

Gaia stepped forward, breathing hard from her impromptu track session. "What gives?" she asked.

Will cocked an eyebrow at her. "I'm sorry?"

"Don't be sorry. Just drop the BS. I'm sick of it," she said, fuming.

"I don't know what you're talking about," he said, his voice taking on a musical lilt.

Gaia rolled her eyes. "And please don't give me the whole Southern gentleman thing because I'm telling you, it's getting old. I see you, you know. I see right through you." She dropped her voice and stepped slightly closer so that she was invading his personal space in a big way. "To be honest? It's not that hard."

"Oh, yeah?" Will asked, leaning in, his face so close to hers, she could feel his breath on her cheek. "And what about you, Miss Mysterious? Gaia Moore, the little girl lost with the troubled past. You don't take crap from anybody, and you don't need anyone, either."

"That's right, I don't," she retorted, suddenly feeling a lot less confident than she sounded. She shook her head. "I don't know why I bothered coming after you."

"Maybe it's because you just can't handle the fact that I won?" Will suggested, his voice high and taunting.

Gaia's eyes narrowed into slits. "Not. Even. A little bit." She took another step forward. Now their noses were practically touching. "You know what they say about glass houses, Will Taylor? And stone throwing? Well, it's true. And let me tell you, your house is glass from top to bottom. You live in a greenhouse. A biodome. You are just like every other guy I've ever met—you need to be stronger, faster, and bigger than me. You need to be the alpha male. But here?" She gestured, sweeping her arm out and away from her body. "Here you're just another muscle-bound supergeek. A big fish in a small pond. But the pond is just brimming with big fish. And it's so obvious."

"What is?" he sneered, seething.

"You just can't handle the fact that your toughest opponent here . . . *is a woman*." She planted her fists on her hips in a superhero pose and glared at him. "And whatever is going on between us, you're letting your own macho crap get in the way.

We *kissed*, Will. And now you're pissed because I'm doing well here? What am I supposed to think about that?"

For a beat he glared right back. In that moment all Gaia was aware of was the sound of their fevered, labored breathing and the gleam of Will's eyes. Listening to the rhythm of the blood pumping inside her ears, all she could think was, *I hate you.*

Then suddenly she was grabbing at him, her hands clutching his waist and drawing him nearer to her. She hadn't thought he could *get* any closer, yet she needed to feel his body pressed against her own. It was as though her hands were operating of their own volition and Gaia's brain was divorced from the process.

It was strange.

Stranger yet was the fact that Will was grabbing her right back. He wrapped one arm around her slender torso and slid his other up her back, burying his hand in the thick of her hair and pulling it free from its elastic. It tumbled down her shoulders and he wove his hands through it, breathing into it. Then he was tracing his lips across her jawline, her neck, her cheek.

And then they were kissing.

Gaia had kissed guys before; in the course of her untraditional adolescence, she'd even managed to have a relationship or two. But this was different somehow. This wasn't romantic, or tender, or emotional. This was raw, primal, and urgent. She thought she might devour Will whole or vice versa.

And that it would be okay.

. . . the hell?

Gaia broke the spell first, pulling away, shaking her head, breathing in tiny short bursts through her nose. She wiped her mouth with the back of her hand, looked away, and hastily wound her hair back up into a messy ponytail at the base of her neck.

She looked up. Will wore a dazed expression. His eyebrows were drawn in confusion, and he was nodding toward the grass, toward nothing in particular.

Slowly he tilted his head up. He made tentative eye contact with Gaia, looking as confused as she felt. He opened his mouth, thought better of it, and shut it again.

Gaia regarded him with a newfound curiosity, as a cat might examine a new brand of catnip. She concentrated on bringing her heart rate down to a regular, non-bionic level.

She was out of words, though. She didn't have anything appropriate to say. "Sorry I just groped you" felt inappropriate, given that she had been as much the gropee as the groper. "What the hell was *that*?" was probably a bit combative, even for her. And, "Hey, why'd we stop?" would really just open a Pandora's box.

Make that Pandora's storage shed. Pandora's costume party of crazy R-rated mind games and unresolved sexual tension.

No, there really wasn't anything to be said. And judging from the look on Will's face—not to mention his abject silence—he wasn't feeling very chatty, either.

Will cleared his throat. "I, uh—"

"I really should," Gaia interjected.

"Right."

"Go."

The two of them turned and walked off in opposite directions, neither one daring to look back.

FEDERAL BUREAU OF INVESTIGATION
TRANSCRIPT—CASE #261, INTERVIEW 1

SUBJECT: <u>Sam Knight</u>

FIELD AGENT: <u>Special Agent Bishop</u>

SAB: Hello, Sam.

SK: (*No reply.*)

SAB: How are you feeling today?

SK: I want to go home.

SAB: Yes, I know you do. I know the other officers explained to you that we're going to get you into your new home just as soon as we can. But in the meantime, this place isn't so bad, is it? Mrs. Habermeyer told me that you get to watch movies at night before bedtime.

SK: My mommy used to read to me.

SAB: Well, maybe if you ask Mrs. Habermeyer, she'd be willing to read to you before bed, too. At least some nights.

SK: But not my mommy because she isn't here anymore. She isn't coming back.

SAB (*Softly.*): No, she's not. (*Sounds of shifting papers.*) Sam, I know it's very hard for you to talk about the man you saw that night and the evening that he hurt your mommy, because the man was very scary, but I want to ask you a few questions about him. Do you think that would be all right? It would really help me if you could tell me a little bit about that night.

SK: I don't remember. (*Sniffling.*) He was big.

SAB: Well, that's a great start. Do you remember how big? Compared to your mother?

SK: Big. Much bigger. And he smelled.

SAH: What did he smell like, Sam?

SK: Like wet.

SAB: Like "wet"? What else? Do you think maybe he smelled like anything else?

SK (*Muffled tears.*): No. Just like wet.

SAB: Okay, that's okay, Sam. I know it was scary. Do you remember where the man came from? Can you tell me anything about that?

SK: I was playing with my truck, and then I heard a noise, and when I came into the kitchen to see where the noise was coming from, I saw the man. And he was sitting on my mommy. And he hurt her. And I wanted to talk to her, but then other people came—the girl with the blond hair and other people. And he ran away. But my mommy was already hurt.

SAB: Did the man say anything to you before he left? Anything at all?

SK: No. (*Louder crying, speech less intelligible.*)

SAB: That's okay. We're finished here. You did a very good job. Thank you so much. You really helped me. We're going to find the scary man who hurt your mom, and we're going to punish him. I promise you. Okay? Now let's go find Mrs. Habermeyer and see about getting some stories for her to read to you.

Gaia had to put the tape aside. Every time she listened to it, Sam's voice reverberated in her ears, sad and small and lost. Yet she wasn't any closer to solving the crime. How did federal agents do this day in and day out? How did they pore over the details of crimes without losing their souls in the process? Did they eventually become hardened? Gaia didn't ever want that to happen to her.

"This is just not getting me anywhere," Gaia groaned, shoving aside the transcript she'd been staring at for the better part of an hour. She'd been reading and rereading the interview between Special Agent Bishop and Sam Knight as though hoping that through her sheer doggedness, some new detail would materialize within the text. That was the only way the interview would be any help, after all. Not to mention, every time that she read it or played the audio file back, the tear in her heart grew just that much deeper. She felt for Sam. She knew what it was like to find your mother dead on the floor one otherwise normal afternoon. It was a sucker punch to the gut, and the feeling never, ever went away. She knew what nightmares were in store for Sam, most likely for the rest of his life. She knew all too well.

"I know," Catherine agreed, not looking up from her keyboard. "He's so traumatized—and can you blame him? I guess I just don't know what more to do." She shrugged. "I'm trying to cross-reference the details that we have with those that are on file in the local criminal records."

"Perfect," Gaia said, slumping down in her seat.

The girls had ventured to the library with Kim in search of a quiet place to catch up on their reading and review the details of the case. Kim just wanted to study. He was keeping plenty busy with his "regular" NAT course load. But Gaia had an ulterior motive.

"There has to be *something*," Gaia insisted, gritting her teeth. "There's always something. We're just missing it. Remember: 'It's not what you see, but what you don't see.' I'm telling you, it's right in front of us, and we're just being chumps." She picked up the transcript, flipping through the pages for the umpteenth time. "Maybe we should talk to Sam ourselves."

"I don't know," Catherine hedged. "Kids are very unreliable witnesses. It takes someone with the proper training to elicit the right information from them."

Gaia jerked her head in Kim's direction. "Well, thankfully, I think we've got just the right person for a crash course."

Kim looked up from the thick textbook he'd been skimming. "Can I help you ladies?" he asked.

Gaia nodded. "We want to go talk to Sam, Ann's son, again. But we know that it's really tricky interviewing kids. Can you give us any tips on how to go about it?"

Kim slid a pencil into the gutter of his book to mark his place and set it aside on the table. Aware of some other trainees in the library shooting them questioning glances, he leaned in and lowered his voice. "There are a few keys," he said.

"Number one, you want to really be sure not to lead them. Kids are fantastic at figuring out what information an adult is trying to get from them. So you want to ask questions as open-endedly as possible. Not, 'Was the man wearing a red sweater?' but, 'What kind of sweater was the man wearing? Do you remember what color it was?'"

"That makes sense," Gaia said. Psychology was truly fascinating to her. On the one hand, it all seemed to be such common sense. But on the other, left to her own devices, she might never have come up with the pointers that Kim was giving her.

"Also, you should avoid asking them the same question twice. Sometimes they think that means they got the answer 'wrong,' so while you're looking for clarity, you're encouraging them to switch their story. Chances are, their first answer is the most accurate one that you're going to get."

"Got it," Catherine said. "Anything else?"

"They're emotional. Sam especially will be, given the circumstances. You want to be as nonthreatening as possible. Scare tactics will not help you pull an answer from a child witness."

Gaia shuddered. "I would never have thought to try to bully a kid."

"I know," Kim said. "But it was worth mentioning, just so that you can be extra-sensitive." He smiled at them sympathetically. "It's a good idea to talk to him. Even if Agent Bishop is the last word in child interviewers, you never know. Sam could take to one of you or suddenly remember something new. There's still a chance, no matter how minuscule, that he'll be able to help you out."

Gaia gathered her books and prepared to go break the news to Bishop and Malloy. Catherine began to shut down her PowerBook.

"That's what I'm hoping," Gaia said to Kim. "Thanks for the leg up."

They were on their way to investigate. It was a long shot, but Gaia had to hope for something, *anything,* to come out of the visit.

She didn't have any shorter shots left.

AUTO-RELEASE

What with all of the talk on the transcript about stories, Gaia had expected Mrs. Habermeyer to be a modern-day Mary Poppins or perhaps a middle-aged woman with graying curls and a soft, rounded figure. Whatever image she had built in her mind, hardly was she expecting to find, on knocking on the front door of the state-sponsored foster care home, a young woman who looked not a day over twenty-four.

"Hello," Mrs. Habermeyer said, opening the front door and stepping aside to allow Gaia, Catherine, and Agent Crane entrance. "I'm Charlotte Habermeyer. I'm the social worker who's been appointed to this home."

"Special Agent Gaia Moore," Gaia said, flashing her badge quickly. She couldn't deny it; she felt a tiny thrill every time she said those words. *Someday it's going to be for real,* she thought. "Thanks for agreeing to see us."

"No problem," Mrs. Habermeyer said. "Anything I can do. I would get personal satisfaction in seeing Sam's mother's murderer behind bars." Her eyes narrowed to tiny slits. "You've met him, of course. So you understand why I feel so personally responsible for his well-being."

"Yes, I do," Gaia said.

"Sam usually likes to spend his days in the playroom in the back," Charlotte said, moving through the front hallway and deeper into the house. "We have a decent toy collection, though I'd like it to be more complete. Our budget's a shoestring; you can't imagine. But thankfully we do get a lot of donations from the community."

They wandered toward the back playroom. It was a nice–enough home, though certainly modest, with a wooden clap-board exterior and large wraparound porch. Inside, the facilities were up to par, if a little worn. But everything was in one piece. *Besides,* Gaia thought grimly, *a lot of these kids are coming from places much, much grimmer.*

"They're such good kids," Charlotte said. "All of them, really. Even the ones who misbehave. They've just had it rough. I just hate to see what they go through."

Gaia and Catherine nodded. Gaia couldn't help but think of her mother and how things might have been different if she'd only lived. She suspected Catherine was thinking about her mother as well—Gaia could only imagine how hard it had been for Catherine to watch someone she loved lose a battle to cancer.

"Sam's been all right. He cries a lot, mostly at bedtime, but that's to be expected. He says his mother used to read to him every night, which I'm more than willing to do, but it's not the same. He's also been having trouble sleeping through the night. He says he has nightmares. But while he's awake, he's just lovely.

A little quiet, but so well behaved. And very polite. I think the worst thing he ever did was to hide his lollipop so I wouldn't take it away."

Gaia's ears pricked up. "Lollipop?"

Charlotte looked at Gaia quizzically. "Yes, the lollipop. The lollipop that the killer gave him. He hid it from me—either he wanted to eat it, or he was embarrassed by it, or he maybe he just thought he would get in trouble for having it. We're not sure. . . ." Her voice trailed off. "You hadn't heard about the lollipop?"

Gaia glanced over at a visibly unnerved Catherine and then frowned. "Yes, we know," she admitted. An image of Sam holding a big lollipop was now visible in her mind. She couldn't believe that she and her partner had failed to mention it in their report. Maybe the shock of the situation and the gruesome crime scene had somehow overwhelmed them enough to make them forget this important piece of information. And because of this error of omission, Bishop had been unable to ask questions about this lead during her interview with Sam. If they had missed this, how could they assume they weren't making other mistakes? How could they trust their skills and their instincts?

"We should talk to him," Gaia said simply, keeping a tight rein on the mishmash of emotions that coursed through her.

Charlotte stopped, standing in the doorway to the back playroom. The room could have been lifted straight out of a seventies tableau: the floor was covered in a green, grass like shag carpet, and two nondescript, beige-ish couches sat kitty-corner along the far and back walls. Between them rested an outdatedly mod coffee table in a brown resin-like material. A battered television sat on a rickety stand across from the longer couch, and next to the television were two tall, simple bookshelves bearing a battle-worn collection of paperbacks.

Sam sat on the longer couch, an action figure abandoned just next to him on the couch. Gaia was stunned to see that during the few days since his mother's murder, Sam's demeanor had altered dramatically. When Ann had first introduced Gaia to her son, he had seemed wide-eyed and friendly. Now he barely glanced up when Charlotte walked Gaia and Catherine over to where he sat, introducing them.

"What do you want?" he asked plaintively, looking up at them blankly. Gaia nearly recoiled at the deep shadows in the hollows of his eyes.

"Gaia and Catherine just want to talk to you for a few minutes, Sam, honey. I'll be in the kitchen."

Sam turned his attention back to his action figure. "Don't worry," Charlotte whispered. "He'll warm to you in a few minutes."

"I'm sure we'll be fine," Catherine said.

"I'll leave you alone with Sam. It's probably better that way. But you can come find me in the kitchen when you're done." She turned and left the room, offering Sam a small wave that he either didn't notice or chose to ignore.

Gaia regarded Sam with a degree of hesitation. She cracked her knuckles nervously. She hadn't had very much experience with children and had always sort of considered them to be another species entirely. She had met her own brother late in life, and though he had taken to her immediately, that had been under entirely different circumstances. Gaia channeled her protective instincts, though, and made her way over to the sofa.

She perched next to Sam, smiling gently. "Hi there," she said. "Can I play *Star Wars* with you?"

Sam peered up at her skeptically. "You're a girl," he said, pouting.

Gaia nodded. "True. So you're telling me a girl can't be Luke Skywalker."

"Luke is a *boy*," Sam pointed out—logically enough, Gaia had to admit.

"My name is Gaia, Sam," she said. She held her hand out for him to shake, and he did, quite solemnly. "And this is my friend Catherine. Do you remember us at all?"

Sam scrunched his face up in concentration. Slowly, realization dawned on his tiny features. "You were at the house that day."

Gaia swallowed hard, trying to force the lump that was working its way up her throat back down. *At least he recognizes us. That has to count for something.*

"And then she went away," he said, looking down at his lap.

"We know about that, Sam," Catherine said. She'd been leaning against the couch. Now she crouched down so that she was face-to-face with him.

"We want to find the man who hurt your mother. And we think we can do it. But we're going to need your help."

Instantly Sam began to cry. "I told the lady. I already told her. When I was at the police station, and I talked to the lady. I don't remember the man."

"That's okay, Sam," Gaia said soothingly. She wanted to reach out and scoop him into her lap, but for now, she'd have to settle for smoothing an errant curl from his sweat-sticky forehead. "If you don't remember, that's fine."

She felt like crying herself. She didn't feel any closer to catching the killer than they'd been the other day at morgue—unless, that was, the lollipop line of questioning actually turned up new information. What were the odds? She hardly wanted to press Sam under the circumstances, but if she wanted to help him, she'd have to.

"I want to help," he said, the tears falling harder now, leaving dark patches on the surface of his green corduroy pants. "But I don't remember."

Gaia's stomach lurched and twisted, a nest of thorns taking root there. She was angry, perhaps angrier than she'd ever been. In all those years that she'd prowled Washington Square Park, busting all the scumbags who raped, mugged, and otherwise assaulted unsuspecting young women, she'd never stopped to consider that there were worse crimes out there waiting to be committed. Yes, she'd seen her mother and her boyfriend killed, but in a way, this was different. This was a *child*. A child who was barely old enough to grasp what had happened, a child who desperately wanted to do anything to bring his mother back. The pitch of Gaia's will and determination rose to another level, a sort of DefCon 5 of sheer, steel resolution. She *would* catch the bastard who had ripped Ann apart.

"Sam, Charlotte told us that the man gave you a lollipop," Gaia prompted, as gently as she could. "How come you didn't tell the police about that before? Were you scared? It's okay if you were," she assured him.

Sam shrugged. "He gave me a red lollipop. Right before . . . I was playing with my truck, and my mommy was in the kitchen."

"Did you see him come in?" Gaia asked.

"No. I was playing, and he came over to see. He asked what I was playing, and he gave me a lollipop. And then he went into the kitchen."

That was where we came in, Gaia thought grimly.

"And you hid the lollipop?" Catherine asked.

"I didn't want to get in trouble," Sam said. "Then I forgot."

"And when you found it, you didn't want to give it to Charlotte?"

Sam looked away. "I thought she would be mad."

"Where is the lollipop now?"

"I ate it," he said. "And then I tried to flush the stick."

That's when Charlotte found it, Gaia surmised. Obviously by then there was no point in dusting for prints.

"We talked to Agent Bishop, the nice lady you spoke with at the police station," Catherine interjected. "She told us that you said that the man smelled 'wet.' Can you tell us if he smelled like anything else?"

Sam shook his head back and forth, sniffling. "No."

Gaia tried to make some sense out of this.

Ann was attacked with a hunting knife. Virginia's got a lot of backwoods. There are a fair amount of hunters and fishermen around here. A fisherman might use a heavy knife to scale and bone his catch. And he probably spent a lot of time around water.

It wasn't a sure bet, though. "Wet" could really mean any number of things to Sam. Not to mention, there were probably a variety of reasons Ann's killer could have smelled or been wet. It was a small, slippery shred of an inkling.

But it was really all they had.

"Sam, that's excellent," Gaia said.

For the first time since Gaia and Catherine had sat down, Sam looked hopeful. "Do you know who it is now?" he asked, his voice small.

"Not quite," Gaia admitted, "but I think we're a little closer."

FEDERAL BUREAU OF INVESTIGATION
REPORT—CASE #261

SUBJECT: <u>Follow-up, Interview #2 (Sam Knight)</u>

SUPERVISORS: <u>Special Agent Hyde, Special Agent Crane, codes B76 and B34</u>

FIELD AGENTS: <u>Gaia Moore and Catherine Sanders*</u>

Contingency basis only

Agents Moore and Sanders met with subject Sam Knight at county foster facility at 14:00 for approx. thirty minutes. Subject was highly distraught at mention of his mother's murder, crying openly when questioned. However, his answers in no way deviated from those given to Special Agent Bishop previously, suggesting that his initial responses, detailed in that interview transcript, are accurate and lucid. He maintained that the suspect smelled "wet" but went on to elaborate that the suspect smelled "like in the winter" (see attached transcript), prompting field agents to speculate that, based on the murder weapon, the wool fibers found on the victim's clothing, and the suggestion of a smell of water, the suspect is in fact either a fisherman or someone who frequently comes in contact with same. Will continue to investigate this thread, conducting interviews at local docks.

Agents were also able to uncover that SK was given a lollipop by the suspect. Suspect is believed to have entered the house, given a lollipop to the boy, and then murdered the victim. Lollipop was red. SK hid lollipop from police and later ate the candy. Lollipop was discovered when stick clogged plumbing at foster center. A conversation with the foster care supervisor confirms this information. Based on a random sample of the major drugstore and supermarket chains within a five-mile radius, it was determined that this was too slim a lead to pursue. Red lollipops are carried by nearly all of the above.

VIRGINIA DEPARTMENT OF GAME AND INLAND FISHERIES
http://www.dgif.state.va.us./fishing/where_to_fish/index.html

VIRGINIA LAKES: Prince Edward/Goodwin Lakes

These two Virginia Department of Conservation and Recreation lakes are the main features of Twin Lake State Park located in Prince Edward County. The park offers campgrounds, cabins, boat ramps, rentals, and swimming. Some fish structures have been built in an effort to concentrate fish for anglers. Grass carp have been stocked to control aquatic vegetation. Both lakes have sunfish, largemouth bass, crappie, and channel catfish. The area is excellent for family outings. Sampling in 1998–2000 indicated that largemouth bass sizes were small and numbers relatively high. This population structure lends itself well to anglers who are interested in catching high numbers of bass as opposed to a few larger fish. The largemouth bass population in both lakes is being managed with a twelve-inch minimum size regulation.

"Make a right here," Gaia said, looking up from the map she'd unfolded in her lap and gesturing to Catherine so as not to miss the turnoff. "I think the dock is just down this road."

Catherine sighed and checked the rearview mirror of her Altima before signaling, braking, and smoothly turning right down a dusty, unpaved road. "I just hope this one turns up some kind of lead—*any* kind of lead," she said wearily.

"Well, it is sort of an educated hunch that we're working from," Gaia reminded her. "But I'm not ready to throw in the towel."

"No, you're right," Catherine agreed. "It's like that first murder you solved in Hogan's Alley—I think it's just a matter of somehow looking long enough and hard enough to connect the dots." She pointed through the windshield at a spot in the distance. "I think that's it." She frowned. "It doesn't exactly look like a large-scale operation." The Altima bounced along the last few paces of the road. Catherine curved around a bend, following signs marked DOCKS, finally coming to a halt in front of a tiny, dilapidated shed that claimed to rent equipment and bait by the hour and the pound, respectively.

"I feel like we've just entered Mayberry," Catherine said.

Gaia had to agree. Looking out toward the water, she could see that the dock was a sorry affair, with soggy planking semi-covered in chipping paint. A few small speedboats were tethered to the dock itself, all of which appeared to have seen better days. The whole area had an air of desolation to it, reminiscent of the inauspicious beginning of any number of horror movies. Did the key to Ann's murder really lie hidden somewhere here? Gaia hoped so. The longer the crime went unsolved, the lower the chances that it ever *would* be solved. Gaia and Catherine were running out of time. "If we're lucky," she replied.

She stepped out of the car purposefully, slamming the door behind her. "Come on."

Gaia strode up to the shed and rapped on the door. After a beat, it opened inward to reveal a large man, face mottled with deep craters and belly hanging low over the strained waist of his jeans. His eyes danced up and down Gaia's slender figure. "Well, hello there," he said, the corners of his mouth turning up in a borderline lecherous grin.

She didn't have time for this. Gaia reached into her inner breast pocket and whipped out her badge. "Sir. Special Agent Gaia Moore, FBI." The leer dissolved from his face and he straightened up before reaching out to shake her hand. "This is my partner, Catherine Sanders. We'd like to ask you a few questions."

"Surely, ma'am. I mean, Agent Moore," the man stuttered, clearly flustered. "My name's Darryl. Darryl Michaels. I run this dock."

"Great," Gaia said. "In that case, maybe you can tell us whether or not you've rented out any of the boats today?"

Darryl nodded, scratching his head with his dirt-caked finger-nails. "There were a few that went out this morning, but they're all back now except one. I can check the logs. Can I ask what this is all regarding?"

"A woman was murdered in Quantico a few days ago," Catherine said. "Ann Knight. We think the killer may have either been a hunter or a fisherman, or he may have known someone who was. So we're just conducting some preliminary interviews, trying to see if anyone knows anything."

"I gotcha," Darryl said. "I didn't know her myself, but maybe someone here does. The regulars are good guys—I'd vouch for them. And I'm sure they'd be happy to talk to ya." He padded back into his office and pulled out a grimy loose-leaf binder. He flipped it open and began scanning down the columns. "Ned Riley's in the last boat out. He's one of my regulars. He'll oblige you if you've got questions."

Catherine reached the flat of her hand out to shield her eyes from the sun. "Is that him?" she asked, pointing through the dust-streaked window to where a man was carefully lining his small motorboat against the dock, winding a thick rope around a wooden post to keep it in place.

Darryl peered out the window to where Catherine was pointing. "Hmm. It surely is. Perfect timing, I'd say."

"Great. Well, we'll go talk to him," Gaia said. "We appreciate the heads-up."

Gaia and Catherine walked briskly down to the end of the dock. Gaia knew it was crucial that they manage to convey authority without startling Ned or putting him on the defensive. She conjured up a tight, professional smile as they reached his boat.

"Hi," Gaia said, pulling out her badge and flipping it open for Ned's benefit. "I'm Special Agent Gaia Moore of the FBI and this is my partner, Catherine Sanders. Ned Riley?"

Ned looked the textbook definition of the phrase "middle-aged man." His hairline was receding and his belly hung over his belt a little. He seemed somewhat surprised to be approached by officers, and even more so when he realized that they knew his name, but he grinned affably and reached out to shake their hands. "That's me," he confirmed. "What can I do for you?"

"We're conducting an investigation," Gaia explained, "and if it's all right with you, we'd like to ask you a few questions."

"Sure," Ned said. "No problem. I can't think of how I'd be able to help you, though. I'm afraid my life's pretty unexciting." He offered a nervous laugh.

"Did you know a woman named Ann Knight?" Gaia asked, getting right down to business.

Ned knit his eyebrows together, thinking it over. "The name does sound awfully familiar. But I can't quite place it."

"She worked as a waitress at a local bar, Johnny Ray's," Catherine explained. "Maybe you saw her there?" A glimmer of recognition flashed across Ned's face. "Oh, yeah. Ann. I do remember her. Young thing but tired. Has a son, right? That she's raising by herself? I used to go to Johnny's once in a while—I remember her telling me about that."

"*Had* a son," Gaia corrected softly. "She was murdered. We're investigating the crime."

Ned looked confused for a moment, then understanding flooded across his face. "Murdered?" He shook his head. "I swear, I don't know what's wrong with people—a nice, hard-working woman like that gets killed." He looked genuinely distressed. "And you don't know who did it, I guess?"

Gaia took a deep breath, not wanting to give anything away. "We have a few leads," she said briefly. "So you say you only spoke to her that one time at the bar?"

Ned nodded. "We weren't friends or anything. I mean, maybe

one or two conversations. I don't go to Johnny's that much. Can't drink the way I used to, if you know what I mean."

Gaia noticed Catherine smiling as though she did know, which Gaia suspected she did not. But for all of Catherine's computer-geek ways, she had a knack for putting people at ease. Gaia thought that technique looked pretty handy. She hoped that with enough practice, she'd be able to do the same.

"I hear you," Catherine said, shaking her head ruefully. "Are you friendly with any of the other regulars who dock here?"

"Kinda," Ned said. "Most everyone here is friendly enough, you know."

"Would you know if anyone here had any contact with Ann?" Gaia prompted.

"Probably not," Ned admitted, "though it is a small enough town. Most of the guys down at this dock are married. So I don't know that they'd be too likely to be palling around with a single mom over at the local tavern."

"But you're not married?" Gaia pressed. Something about Ned's total willingness to speak with her rubbed her the wrong way. This was the last dock they were visiting this afternoon, and almost everyone else they'd encountered had been defensive and resentful, displeased to be questioned. On the other hand, Ned seemed almost eager to be talking to the FBI. As if he were trying to *prove* he had nothing to hide.

As if he were hiding something.

"No, ma'am, I'm not. Had a sweetheart in high school, but . . . well, it didn't work out," he said, blushing.

"Did you ever see anyone else talking to Ann at the bar? Maybe another guy? Someone who came in often?" Catherine asked.

"Nope. Like I said, I've only been once or twice. I would never have noticed anything like that."

"Well," Gaia said brusquely, "I believe we have all of the information that we need. You've been very helpful, and we do appreciate it."

"Really?" Ned said. "You're sure? Because I would truly be happy to do what I can. I hate the thought of anyone hurting that poor woman. You please do be sure and give me a call if anything else comes up that you want to ask me about."

Gaia couldn't believe it when he borrowed her pencil and scratched out his phone number. Was it too much to imagine that he was such a sincerely Good Samaritan that he was dying to remain in contact, just in case something new came up? Or was he desperately unhinged and definitely hiding something? She really had no way of knowing . . . until something happened that made the very hairs on the back of her neck stand at attention. It was a small detail, but Gaia didn't miss it.

When Ned took the pencil from her, she watched him write out his phone number.

She watched him write it out with his left hand.

Fortune-teller magic

Nothing helped Will clear his mind like running outdoors did. He could do the job on a treadmill if he had to, sure, but it wasn't the same thing. The contained space of a gym didn't give him the same charge that actual, honest-to-goodness fresh air brought with each breath, each surefooted stride. In fact, one of the only things that he didn't like about his hometown was how incredibly, unbearably humid it became over the summer. The humidity rendered it nearly suffocating to run outside at any time other than the earliest hours of the morning. Of course, all of that practice had turned out to be a pretty good thing, considering where he'd ended up. The FBI officials hadn't been kidding when they'd said that their program challenged people on an intense physical level, and he didn't think that the FBI had much use for people who liked to sleep in.

Thump, thump, thump, thump. His feet hit the ground at a casual lope, just enough to get his heart going and to burn off some of the energy from the day. Crazy, he knew, given how hard they were pushed physically, to voluntarily choose to push himself even harder, but he honestly couldn't help himself. People asked him—they asked him *all the time*—whether or not he minded not going out for the Olympics. Whether he felt that he'd missed out. The answer was yes. And no. No, because ultimately, he sincerely believed that working as a federal agent had more social value than competing for titles. Yes, because the competitor inside him damn well liked his titles.

Today, for instance, he'd had a terrible stint out at the shooting range. Missed his target by a mile. It bugged him because they were monitoring his progress and because *he* was monitoring his progress. Annoying. So there was that tension.

Then there was the fact that Kim seemed to be looking at him differently ever since the handwriting analysis clinic. He could hardly believe that someone as well trained as Kim could put so much stock into that exercise. Handwriting analysis? It was David Copperfield BS—even Catherine had said as much. And Kim, of all people, with his advanced psych degrees and his amazing insight into "people" should have known that. All of that stuff about him having a split personality? Based on the way he crossed his *t*'s? Ridiculous. Not to mention, they had to function as a team, the four of them, which would never happen if Kim was using fortune-teller magic to appraise Will's personality.

What if Kim's suspicion spread to the rest of the team?

What if it spread to Gaia?

Gaia. Absently Will allowed his mind to wander back to her, to their kiss—their *kisses*. It had happened twice now, the kissing, one on the day she'd been sure she was going to leave and then again yesterday. What was that about? Sure, he'd thought about kissing Gaia basically from the moment he'd laid eyes on her. Any sane, straight man would have. She was stop-in-your-tracks-and-stare gorgeous. The kind of gorgeous that reduced most men to babbling fools. But it was more than that, even. She was sophisticated and worldly in a way that Will was not. She'd been places, that much was obvious. But wherever she'd been, she sure didn't want to talk about it.

How had they gotten to this bizarre, unidentified place? When he'd picked her up the other day in his car, they'd talked, more personally than usual. The kiss had happened organically, and he had assumed that there was something, some semblance of a relationship, brewing. And then . . . her contingency badge. For days he'd been so irked with her. Jealous of her. On some level he knew she deserved it thoroughly, but that didn't mean he was any less envious. Will Taylor had never been known for being a gracious loser. So the badge had necessarily gotten in the way of whatever was happening between them. Until the sparring yesterday.

When they were paired up for sparring, he'd been determined to beat her down. He could take her, he knew, and in that forum it was not only considered legitimate to do so, it was downright expected of him. But something had happened when her skin touched his, some electrical charge. The competitor in him wanted to kick her ass, but the Y chromosome in him had entirely different reasons for being tangled on top of her, limbs intertwined. It was confusing. And kissing her hadn't helped him make any sense of it. But it sure had been nice.

For once running wasn't helping him to come to any conclusions. He vowed to put Gaia out of his mind, at least for the immediate future.

"Hey."

Will looked up and blinked. Was it possible—a mirage, here in the woodlands of Quantico? He rubbed his eyes. One minute the image of Gaia pummeling him was playing through his mind, and suddenly here she was, in the flesh, a vision in track pants and a T-shirt. Her hair was pulled back off her face in a messy ponytail and her face shone with exertion. Clearly she'd had the same idea he had. He nearly tripped and went flying, he was so surprised to see her.

Get it together, he commanded himself. *No need to go weak-kneed just because a pretty girl materializes out of nowhere.*

"Hey there," he said calmly, offering her a friendly smile. So she was still talking to him after their impromtu make-out session. That was probably a good sign. Even if it never happened again—and he wasn't at all sure how he felt about *that* prospect—at least they could talk to each other. He decided he'd take her cues from her. If she wasn't going to bring it up, then neither was he.

Two can play at that game, he decided. That was, if it was a game.

Of course it is. It always *is,* he reasoned. *It's always a game, and I can always win.*

"Did you just come out?" he asked.

Gaia nodded. They were keeping a steady pace but not going full force, so conversation was easy. "Yeah, Catherine and I had a rough day. Did a lot of questioning on Ann's case, didn't really get anywhere. One lead. But who knows. Anyway, I had some, uh, tension to burn off." On the word *tension,* she glanced at him sideways. It did not go unnoticed.

"It always helps me clear my mind," Will agreed. "I love it."

"Right, I figured, what with the Olympics thing," Gaia said. She paused, as if considering whether or not to ask her next question. "Were your parents disappointed that you decided not to compete? Or excited that you were going into the FBI?" When Will didn't answer right away, she went on. "Not to pry."

"No, it's not prying," Will said, considering. "What about yours? Your parents, I mean. The FBI is pretty intense. Do *they* worry?"

"My dad . . . knows the score," Gaia said. If she realized that he hadn't answered her question, she decided not to press. "He does this kind of stuff, too." He could tell she was being deliberately vague. "And my mom . . ." Gaia trailed off.

Will didn't know Gaia very well; he suspected no one did—she kept herself pretty well guarded—but it was easy enough to see how difficult this was for her. She bit her lip, then began again. "My mom died," she said, exhaling as if from the sheer weight of the confession.

"I'm sorry," Will said.

"It was a long time ago," Gaia said. "I'm learning to deal. I'm trying, anyway. To be a little more open with people." She turned and looked directly at Will, making eye contact and infusing her words with meaning.

Unsure how to reply, Will had to content himself with replying at all. They ran along in comfortable silence for a few paces, Will enjoying the sunshine and the breeze in his hair. He could hear leaves rustling and branches crackling underneath their feet, could match his pace to Gaia's measured breaths. It was very peaceful, he realized. Normally he preferred running alone. But this . . . this was pleasant. He could get used to this.

"Are you busy later tonight?" Gaia asked, breaking into his thoughts.

"Why?" he asked mischievously. "Are you asking me out on a date?"

She snorted.

Will grinned. She was so predictable. "No, of course not. That surely would never happen, Miss Moore. I apologize."

"It's Special Agent Moore to you," she retorted.

"Touché," he said with a wink. "So, not a date. In which case I have to ask just what, exactly, you had in mind."

"Nothing crazy. Catherine wanted to get a group together to go to Johnny Ray's," she said. "Just to blow off some steam. She didn't seem to get that *this* is how I blow off steam, but I told her I'd meet her and I'd see who else wanted to go. I think Kim's coming and his roommate. What do you think?"

"I'd be happy to join y'all," Will said easily. He edged closer to Gaia as they ran, elbowing her in the side teasingly. "On one condition."

"What's that?" Gaia asked suspiciously. "I should warn you, I really don't do conditions."

"You just have to promise me that under no circumstances is this to be considered a date."

Gaia rolled her eyes. "You're hilarious," she said, deadpan. But she was smiling.

To Will, that was a start.

WILLINGNESS TO FURTHER THE INVESTIGATION

If Gaia was worried that there was any lingering expectation of romance on her non-date with Will, ten seconds inside Johnny

Ray's killed that concern. The place was doing a brisk enough business, but it was mostly due to the patrons who turned out from some five towns over to enjoy the weekly gay night. Gaia and her friends had been at Johnny Ray's for all of twenty minutes before Kim sauntered off to make "polite chitchat" (his term, not Gaia's) with a student he'd met at the bar the week before. Watching Kim work his mojo on the slender, attractive boy, Gaia had to smile. At least some people knew how to flirt. All she knew how to do was to bicker, spar, and kiss and run.

She shook her head. What the hell had that been, that moment with Will yesterday? One minute she was *infuriated* with him, wanting to wipe the floor with his silly grin, and then the next minute he was on top of her, pinning her down . . . and instead of thinking about escape tactics, all she could think was, *I wonder how it would feel to kiss him right now.* It was ridiculous. Just plain ridiculous. If she wanted to succeed at Quantico, she would have to apply herself and focus every last measure of reserve on her studies. She couldn't be fantasizing about kissing random guys or getting involved with them.

"For you, madame."

Gaia looked up as Will set a tall, cold pint of beer down on the bar next to her. "Thanks," she mumbled.

"No worries, darlin', I'm happy to oblige. Besides, your gracious appreciation is thanks enough," he said, gently mocking her.

Gaia smiled. "Sorry," she said, appreciating his laugh at her expense. "It was very thoughtful of you to buy me a beer. I'll get the next round—if we stay that long."

"Right, best to keep things even," he agreed. "I'd hate for this to in any way resemble a date."

"It's not a date," Gaia insisted. "We came with a carfull of friends."

"All of whom have conveniently disappeared," Will pointed out. Kim still stood in the far corner with his student, while Catherine was having what looked to be an intense conversation with Tate over by the bathroom.

"Listen," Gaia said, straightening up and scowling with annoyance. "I know you're, like, some big-time athlete who is used to having women fall at your feet right and left, but the thing is that yesterday . . . that . . ."

"Kiss," Will filled in.

"Yes, that kiss," Gaia said. *"Both* of the kisses," she corrected, "were a mistake. I have no idea what happened."

"And you're saying I do? That I somehow wanted it?" Will challenged.

"Well, one of us did," Gaia insisted, growing frustrated. Her voice rose an octave. "And I don't think it was the me of us."

"Ms. Moore, I'm sorry to say it, but attention to detail is clearly not your strong suit," Will interjected. "Or if you're trying to convince me that you *happened* to *accidentally* trip and fall on my lips, then I'm going to have to—"

"Do we have to get into this?" Gaia asked. She was so confused by her feelings for Will, the last thing she needed right now was a Serious Talk.

Will rolled his eyes. "Why are you hell bent on avoiding—"

103

"Shhh," she said, cutting him off and waving her hand impatiently. "One second."

"What?" Will asked, baffled as to what she was looking at.

Gaia leaned forward and stared. Was it possible? Could it really be him?

No. No way.

In the midst of the crowd, she was sure that she saw Ned Riley. He was wearing a baseball cap and a cleaner shirt than the one he'd had on at the dock that afternoon, but it was Ned, no doubt about it. Gaia's spine tingled. She'd been suspicious of Ned and his incredible willingness to further the investigation all along. What the hell was wrong with a guy who didn't even get upset or offended at being questioned—basically being told he was suspected of murder? But Ned had been pleasant, even eager to help.

And now he was here. At Johnny Ray's.

Ned had told Gaia that he had been into the bar *maybe once or twice*. Now he was back in here? Either he had lied to Gaia about the amount of time he spent at Johnny Ray's or seeing her and talking to her had jogged his memory and piqued his interest. Either way, he was pretty freaking dim to be coming to Johnny's just hours after being questioned about Ann's murder.

This was bad news.

Gaia glanced back at Ned to make sure he was sufficiently distracted. She needn't have worried: he was busy pouring from a pitcher of something that looked light-beer-colored and laughing at something one of his friends had just said. Without another word to Will, she marched over to the far end of the bar, where Kelly stood. Gaia was hoping that Will wouldn't follow her—the last thing she needed was him breathing down her neck and making her nervous while she worked. She was already pumped up enough. The sight of Ned immediately sparked a rush of adrenaline in Gaia, which she was trying hard to keep under control.

"What's up, doll?" Kelly asked, pleased to see Gaia. Picking up on the expression on Gaia's face, however, she changed her tone. "You've got business on your mind," she realized.

Gaia jerked her head in Ned's direction. "Do you know that guy?" she asked.

Kelly looked at Ned and then back at Gaia. "Yeah, of course, that's Ned Riley. He comes in here all the time. Why?" she asked.

He comes in here all the time, Gaia thought, reeling inwardly as though she'd just been hit with a block of concrete. Ned had lied to them. He had lied to them, plain and simple. Which bumped him way higher up on her list of suspects. "Did he known Ann?" she asked.

Kelly nodded, her eyebrows arching nervously. "Yeah, as a matter of fact, babe, he was real sweet on Ann. Had a crush on her, big-time. Used to come in and try to convince her to go out with him, you know, almost every day. But she always said no. Said the only boy for her was Sam." She grew somber. "It really is a shame, what happened to her." She glanced up, as if suddenly startled. "Wait a minute. You're not thinking that Ned had something to do with Ann's murder, are you? I mean, I can't pretend to know him that well, but I just don't believe that boy would be able to hurt a fly."

Gaia sighed and ran her fingers through her hair. "Kelly," she said, shaking her head ruefully, "you know I can't say anything about that."

"USED" TO THIS

Gaia's doubts led her and Catherine back to the ME's office early the next morning. She told Catherine they were just exploring a hunch, which she would expound on if and when it looked to be coming to fruition.

"I pulled all of the photos from the autopsy," Ben said to Gaia, handing her a thick manila envelope.

"Excellent," Gaia said, opening the envelope and taking out the photos. Even in replica, the images of Ann's mutilated body hit her like a truck. Would she ever get used to this?

Did she *want* to get to the point where she was "used" to this?

"What are you looking for?" Alice asked.

"I guess I just want to see the knife wounds again," Gaia explained. "We were at the docks the other day and talked to some guys. I know we"—she indicated Ben, Alice, and Catherine—"talked about the perp using a hunting knife. But I wonder if it wasn't a fishing knife. There are some that are multi-purpose, and some of the sharper boning tools could have left the same size wound."

Alice nodded thoughtfully. "Of course," she agreed. "And a fisherman would have more occasion or reason to smell 'wet,'" she added, confirming Gaia's theories. "Like Sam describes in his interview."

"Right," Catherine said, sounding enthusiastic to at last have an honest-to-God lead. "So what were you thinking, Gaia? That we'd head back to the docks and ask some more questions?"

"Definitely," Gaia said, setting her mouth in a thin, tight line. "I, for one, have a few questions to ask Ned Riley."

THE SOFT-SPOKEN TYPE

"Back so soon?" Darryl asked, offering Gaia and Catherine a slightly less slimy grin than he had yesterday afternoon. "Should I be flattered or worried?"

"You said that Ned Riley was one of your regulars," Gaia reminded him. "Is he here today?"

Darryl shook his head apologetically. "No, ma'am," he said. "Tomorrow and then again during the weekend. Did you have more questions for him?"

"We have a few questions," Catherine confirmed. "But maybe you can help us."

"Anything I can do, ladies, you know that," Darryl replied nervously.

"You rent equipment, right?" Gaia asked. "To your clientele?"

He nodded. "I do. Although quite a few of them have their own equipment that they bring with them when they come."

"We're assuming that most fishermen use knives to gut and clean their catches," Gaia said. "Would you confirm that?"

"Yes, they do," Darryl said. "Most everyone here uses the model that I rent out, even if they own a knife. It's the most popular model." He wandered deeper into the shed, disappearing momentarily before reemerging brandishing a box. He held the box out to Catherine and Gaia. "It's the Yukon Bay double, model SC-42. Just came out this year. I stock up on good-quality materials," he said. "You need to if you're serious about fishing."

Gaia thought that people who were serious about fishing were also probably serious about docking at higher-end facilities, but she bit her tongue. Darryl was actually being pretty helpful and there was no need to piss him off. She glanced at Catherine, who was scribbling the name and make of the knife into a notebook. She hoped Catherine didn't mind the fact that she was so aggressively taking the lead on this case. Especially since she wasn't planning to step off or back off at any point. Oh, well. Catherine didn't seem like the soft-spoken type. If she had any issues, Gaia had to assume that she'd hear about them. She turned back to Darryl. "I'm assuming we can borrow this model?" she asked.

Darryl looked surprised, and not pleasantly so, but to his credit, he didn't protest. "Of course," he said, regaining his composure. "Take it for as long as you need."

"Thanks," Gaia said, taking the case from him and folding it under her arm. "We just need to run some tests. But we'll bring it back as soon as we're done."

With a wave and a final "thank you," Gaia and Catherine were ready to go. They had to hit the labs again.

SCANNED:

YUKON BAY DOUBLE HUNTING KNIFE, SC-42

PHOTOS A-12, A-14

Results of scans indicate that victim's wound pattern, size, and shape are consistent with the pattern of infliction of the YB SC-42. Percent possibility that murder weapon was YB SC-42 determined to be **85.4%.**

"Interesting," Agent Bishop said, tapping her pencil on the surface of her desk and looking at Gaia with a gleam of respect in her eyes. "You drew up the list of questions together?"

Gaia nodded. "Catherine and I put it together after the lab came back with the results of the scan of the autopsy photos and the sample knife. The cross-referencing matched them within 85.4 percent."

Agents Crane and Hyde nodded from their respective posts at the door of the office, confirming Gaia's claim.

After Gaia and Catherine had received the results of the lab scan, they'd realized that there was no denying Ned Riley was their top suspect. They couldn't overlook the fact that he had been incredibly friendly to them when they'd first questioned him—too friendly—and that, most glaringly, he had definitely lied about his relationship with Ann. Finally there was the fact that his fishing equipment, which he stored at the dock, was consistent with the murder weapon. The two of them had immediately paid a visit to Agent Bishop, who'd sent out a team to pick up Ned from his home and bring him in for questioning. While they were gone, Gaia and Catherine pulled together a list of questions to ask, which they'd then brought to Agent Bishop to vet.

"It looks great," Bishop said, smoothing her hair out of her face. "Very good cop/bad cop." She smiled at them despite the gravity of the situation. "Which one of you is the good cop?"

"I am," Catherine said. "Since Gaia was the one who actually caught him in the lie, we decided she'd have a harder time playing nice."

"Don't worry," Gaia assured Bishop. "I can be the bad cop and still maintain my objectivity."

"Good to know," Bishop said sharply. "Because he's here, in the main office, in holding room one. You get one run-through with Crane and Hyde, just so you're more familiar with the questions. But then you're on."

Gaia swallowed, eyes widening. She hadn't expected to be "on" so soon. She hoped she was ready. *I'll have to be*, she reminded herself. *There's no room for error here.*

She turned to Catherine. "I guess it's time, then."

PLAYING "BAD COP"

"Hi, Ned," Catherine began, smiling nicely. "Thanks for coming in to talk to us."

"I didn't exactly have much of a choice," he said, eyes darting across the room like a caged animal's. "Even though I'm not sure what you want from me. I told you, I sure didn't kill Ann. I'd never hurt anybody."

He looked like he was starting to feel claustrophobic. Gaia could relate. The small holding room was airless and poorly ventilated, little more than a closet, with a long mirror on the wall that was actually a one-way window. Crane and Hyde were watching the questioning from the opposite side of the glass. It made her self-conscious. The floor and walls were white, and the room was lit with dim fluorescent tubes. She felt disoriented and out of place. Playing "bad cop" was going to require some serious mental effort. She was glad that Catherine had decided to start the questioning off on a cheerier note.

"Well, we appreciate it, regardless," Catherine said. "And we just want to ask you a few questions."

"You already did, over at the dock," he reminded them, not sounding petulant, but rather matter-of-fact.

"It seems to me that over at the dock, you told us you'd be happy to help out in any way possible," Gaia reminded him with a slight edge to her tone. "Does that ring a bell?"

Ned glanced down at the table sheepishly. "Yes, I recall that. And I meant it."

"Then you'll just have to answer our questions," Gaia snapped. Was this "bad cop"? If so, she thought she could handle it.

"You may remember that we told you Ann Knight was murdered," Catherine said, softening her tone to take the edge off Gaia's words. "We need to know where you were that evening."

Ned's eyes widened in dismay. "I told you, I had nothing to do with it!" he repeated, fervent and intense. "I would never hurt anyone—but certainly not her."

"Funny," Gaia said dryly. "You seem pretty passionate about that fact. But I *thought* you said you barely knew her."

"Well, I do—I did," Ned stammered. "Like you said, I just saw her at the bar once or twice."

You're a liar, Ned Riley, Gaia thought, adrenaline humming underneath her skin. *And I'm going to prove it.*

"It's interesting that you say that," Gaia began casually. "That you say you don't really go to Johnny Ray's that often. Because—"

"Where did you say you were on the evening of Ann's murder?" Catherine cut in, interrupting. She shot Gaia a look that Gaia instantly identified. *Please don't blow it,* the look said. *That's our money shot. Don't blow it this early in the game.* "If you could answer that for us, it'd be a huge help."

"I was playing poker. You can call my friend Bill. Bill Braeburn. We play together every Thursday. He'll vouch for me."

"I can call him," Gaia said gruffly. She whipped out a small notepad and a mechanical pencil. "Give me his number and I'll be happy to do that."

"Five-five-five, three-seven-oh-three," Ned recited dutifully.

Gaia had to admit, Ned seemed nervous, but not nearly as defensive as she would have expected. He wasn't acting like he had anything to hide. She'd known quite a few people in her lifetime with something to hide, so she knew what that sort of behavior looked like. But then, why had he lied about knowing Ann and about going to Johnny's? Even if he wasn't Ann's murderer, something wasn't on the up-and-up here.

Gaia stood from her seat and stretched. "Great," she said, almost taunting Ned. "I'll just go check on that now. Catherine, you're okay here, right?"

Catherine nodded. "We're fine," she confirmed.

Gaia stepped outside of the holding room and sighed, trying to shake off some of the tension she'd felt while conducting the interview. Even just those few questions she'd managed to squeak out had drained her. Running this check on Ned's alibi would be a welcome break.

She headed down the hall toward the nearest office phone, but she hadn't made it more than ten paces before she was stopped by Crane sprinting toward her. The urgent expression on his face was in stark contrast to his usual buttoned-down demeanor.

"What's up?" she asked.

"Your suspect," Crane said, breathing hard. "He has an alibi?"

Gaia shrugged. "You heard him yourself through the window. Says he was playing poker."

"Well, you should still confirm it." Crane took a deep breath, steeling himself. "Although since he's been here with you for the last hour, then there's a good chance he didn't do it."

Gaia looked at him strangely. "Why do you say that?"

"Because there's been another murder."

COPYCAT CRIME

Gaia placed a quick call to Ned's poker buddy before racing back into the interrogation room. "Ned," she said quietly. "It looks like your story checks out."

Ned looked at her, his face relaxing instantaneously. "Thank God. You called Bill?"

Gaia nodded quickly. "Yes," she admitted. "Can you excuse us for a second?" She gestured to Catherine to step out into the hall. Once the door was shut behind them, she explained. "Crane says there's been another murder. Same MO. Happened in the last thirty minutes."

"This means it's a serial killer," Catherine said, distressed. "That or a copycat crime. Damn." She clenched her fists in frustration. She had obviously really been hoping that they had their man.

They stepped solemnly back into the questioning room.

"Am I . . . free to go?" Ned asked tentatively.

Gaia turned to him. "We're willing to believe that you aren't the killer," she said tersely. "But there's one thing I still need to know. Why did you lie about knowing Ann? I saw you at Johnny Ray's. I know you're a regular there. Kelly told me you had a crush on Ann. But you told me that you only went in there once or twice."

Ned's cheeks colored. "I did lie. I'm sorry. It's just I panicked. I couldn't believe it when you told me Ann had been killed. Kelly was right—I did have kind of a thing for her."

"And you thought it would look bad? Your crush?" Catherine guessed gently.

Ned nodded. "Although I know that lying to you looks worse. It just . . . happened. I didn't mean for it to happen—it just did. I would never, never have done anything to hurt Ann. I was a little disappointed when Ann wasn't interested in me—and she made it clear that she wasn't," he said, wincing a bit. "But I understood that she was pretty busy taking care of her son—you know, like never wanting to go out when she could stay home with him and stuff—and I respected her for that."

"We understand," Gaia said. "But this whole thing would have been a lot easier if you had just told us the truth."

"I swear, that's the only lie I told," he insisted. "And I know it's a big one. But it's the only one. And I meant it when I told you I would do anything I could to help in the future. Honestly, say the word, and I'll do it. I want to catch this guy as badly as you do."

"I hope you mean that," Gaia said grimly, "because we may just have to take you up on that offer. But for now," she said, crossing back to the door and pulling it open for him, "you're free to go."

CAPABILITIES AS AN AGENT

As soon as they'd discharged Ned, Gaia and Catherine ran back to Bishop and Malloy's office. Based on the expressions on the agents' faces, both had heard the news.

"There's been another one," Gaia said, breathless.

Malloy nodded. "Details almost identical to the first killing. Either a copycat or a serial killer in the making."

"Can we get the file?" Gaia asked, willing herself not to be impatient. "We want to get down to the crime scene right away."

Malloy shook his head, his dark eyes gleaming. "While it's commendable that you're so eager to get going, I'm going to have to refuse your request," he said.

"On what grounds?" Gaia asked, her eyes narrowing into small slits. *Keep cool,* she reminded herself. *Malloy is looking for any sign that you can't control your emotions.*

"It seems to me that you both have to be at target practice in" he glanced at his watch casually—"fifteen minutes. And as good as I think you both are, there's really no way you can be in two places at once."

"What?" Gaia demanded, fuming, all attempts at maintaining her composure gone. "That's insane." She looked to Bishop for backup, but the woman just shook her head quickly. Gaia would get no support there.

"Look, Gaia, I'm glad you're on top of this investigation, but when we gave you your contingency badge, we told you that you would have to keep up with your regular program. Which means that you're going to have to hit the firing range with the rest of the trainees. *Before* you visit the crime scene. Crane and Hyde can handle the evaluation, and they'll fill you in later."

Gaia opened her mouth to respond but changed her mind after observing the look on Malloy's face. She knew that he had his doubts about her capabilities as an agent, and she really didn't need to give him any more ammunition to use against her.

"Fine," she said quickly. She turned to Catherine. "Let's go."

A THIRD-PERSON PERSPECTIVE

Catherine might not have had Kim's expertise on the subject of psychology, but she was a pretty good judge of character. If she hadn't thought she had some sort of talent at reading people, she never would have even considered a career with the FBI. After all, one wrong judgment in the field, and you were either dead or severely injured. There was absolutely no room for error among this group. Thankfully, she thought, she wasn't too incredibly terrible at reading people.

Take Gaia, for instance. Gaia clearly had some boundary issues. It was plain to see that the girl hadn't had a lot of close bonds growing up, and she didn't especially like to open up to people. Catherine could dig that. The only person she'd really shared herself with was her ex-boyfriend, Matt, and God, did she ever miss him. Anyway, she wasn't necessarily looking to bond with Gaia over slumber parties and makeover tips—but she thought she could at least get a handle, just a third-person perspective, on what made Gaia tick. And, for that matter, what didn't.

The number-one thing that did *not* make Gaia tick (after, of course, swapping saccharine tales of puppy love with her bestest girlfriends in the world) was guns. Gaia hated guns. She probably didn't realize it, but she flinched every time she walked past the firing range, and even though she did her best to hide it, she grimaced every time she had to touch one. She even hated the paint-filled guns that they used for their practical applications course, and Catherine figured there was probably some deep-seated phobia associated with the real ones they'd been issued for this investigation. So no, Catherine had no idea what it was about guns that skeeved Gaia out so badly, but whatever it was, she hoped Gaia got over it soon. Because what would have been a fine release at the firing range, a great way to shake off some tension before they had to hit yet another gruesome crime scene, had instead wound Gaia up so tightly, she was practically grinding her teeth down to small nubs as they made their way to the site of the murder.

"Have you gone through the file?" Catherine asked, hoping to bring Gaia back to the case. Or at the very least to distract her.

Gaia nodded, sitting adjacent to Catherine in the passenger seat of the Altima. "Yeah. Stats are really almost exactly the same as in the first case. Margaret Johnson, thirty-four, single mother of one young boy. Not a waitress, though. She worked as a cleaning lady for a local maid service. Kept long hours." She paused. "It sounds awful."

"Same type of murder?" Catherine asked.

"Her throat was slit, just like Ann's," Gaia said, reading aloud. "Almost all the way through. They took her to the morgue, but they took pictures that we can look at later. And we'll go to the morgue again."

"This is right near where Ann lived," Catherine observed, flicking on her blinker to signal an upcoming turn.

"Yeah," Gaia agreed. "Because the bastard preys on women who don't have enough money to live anywhere nicer." She sighed. "Crane and Hyde already swept the scene—fingerprints, photos, and fiber samples. I don't know what there is for us to do at this point, especially since they already took the body in. But it couldn't hurt to look."

"No," Catherine agreed, appreciating Gaia's thoroughness for what felt like the umpteenth time. "It certainly couldn't."

Gaia

It's always something, right?

I'm sorry, I don't mean to be flippant—it's just that Catherine and I are, at least in part, responsible for bringing a woman's—*two women's*—killer to justice, and it's always, always something. We've got no new evidence and we can't catch a break, and if I can't laugh about it, I think I'm going to lose my mind.

For most of my adolescence, I thought I had it pretty rough. My mom was dead and my father was constantly missing in action, and I was basically always on the run from someone who really wanted to harm me.

Kim agrees with Nietzsche's theory that whatever doesn't kill you only makes you stronger, and I suppose it's true. God knows I probably wouldn't have considered the luxurious lifestyle of vigilante justice if it hadn't been for my totally messed-up upbringing. So I guess, in some twisted way, missing my parents and being raised on my own are what led me to the place that I'm at now. Finally it feels like I have a sense of personal fulfillment. So maybe it would be wrong to complain. But that never stopped me before.

Well, it's stopping now. Because now I truly realize that while no one is going to mistake my upbringing for a picturesque, idyllic fairy tale, the fact remains that other people have it worse. Or at the very least, they sure as hell have it just as bad.

Sam, for example. He saw his mother sliced up on the floor, eyes open in that blank death stare, and the only thing he has from that day is the memory of a red lollipop and someone who smelled "wet." And let me tell you, that memory, those images . . . they'll haunt him until his dying day. Trust me on this one. Now what does Sam have to look forward to? A string of foster-home placements; a big, honking pile of abandonment issues; and, if he's really lucky, a heap of questions about his parents that no one will ever really be able to answer to his real satisfaction.

It was bad enough when it was just Sam. I could live a lifetime without ever having to encounter that sort of grief etched across the face of a child. I was determined to catch his mother's killer and make him pay. But now there's another. And if it's not the same *exact* guy, it's someone who's damn close to the first case. It doesn't matter. He's not going to get away with it.

Neither one of them is.

I'm going to have to live the rest of my life without a mother. And so is Sam, and so is Timmy, the son of the most recent victim. Timmy's lollipop was grape. Same style, though: no frills, penny-candy style. He hadn't eaten it yet, so we were able to take it as evidence. Timmy has a grape lollipop but not a mother. Does it make me angry? No.

It makes me *furious*. But it's okay. I'll get the bad guy in the end.

I always do.

High-speed, wireless city

Gaia was lying on her back on her bed, staring at the ceiling, when Catherine bounded into their dorm room. Catherine's upbeat mood clashed with Gaia's emotions dramatically; she'd been flopped across her mattress for the better part of an hour now, replaying the crime scene in her head. The latest victim, Margaret Johnson, had been stabbed in her bedroom while her son was downstairs watching TV. Thankfully, Timmy hadn't heard the killer come in. Less thankfully, he had found his mother dead, approximately half an hour after the estimated time of death. At age five, Timmy had known about 911. But that hadn't saved his mother, and therefore it really didn't do much for Gaia's mood.

"You're cheery, considering," she observed. "What gives?"

Catherine sat on the edge of her bed, gently depositing her PowerBook down next to her. "I was at the library, working," she said. "I may be on to something."

"Yeah?" Gaia asked. "Something related to that?" She tilted her head in the direction of the PowerBook.

Catherine nodded, flushed with excitement. "I'm not sure, but I think I've managed to replicate the coding of a typical search engine to create a superpower filter. Like Google on steroids."

"What can it do?" Gaia asked, sitting up and leaning forward, suddenly taking much more interest in Catherine's news.

"Um, basically anything we want it to do," she said, eyes twinkling. "Check it out: we put in the names of any two people, and the filter will pull up any and all points of commonality. Birthplace, places of employment, education, residence. I think it'll be helpful in connecting the dots between Ann, Margaret, and . . . well, if there's anyone else, we can figure out how she fits into the picture."

"I liked everything you said until that point," Gaia replied. "I refuse to think that there will be anyone else. Now that we know this is a pattern crime, it should help us narrow our search a little. I mean, before, it really could have been anyone. But I think when it comes to patterns, the scope necessarily becomes more limited."

"Exactly," Catherine said. "I think this could be a big help."

"It sounds that way," Gaia agreed. "But I'm not sure I get how this is better than a regular search engine."

"It's more specialized," Catherine explained. "You can input as much information as you want and it will filter through it, as opposed to something like Google, which can only process short strings of information. Also, it's plugged into LexisNexis and other secure databases. So we get better dirt than we would from something mainstream."

"Good call," Gaia said, feeling one of the first true glimmers of hope that she'd experienced since they were first put on the case.

"I scheduled some lab time for us," Catherine said. "Over at Eaton. We can camp out by the computer terminals. High-speed, wireless city. No one will bother us."

"Sounds good," Gaia agreed. "How about after dinner?"

"Perfect," Catherine said. "In the meantime, I guess, just cross your fingers."

"If that's what it's come to," Gaia said, "we're in worse trouble than I thought."

TECH-WHIZ BRAINCHILD

After her conversation with Catherine, Gaia was feeling energized enough to throw on her running clothes and hit the trail. She didn't want to admit it, but on some level she was looking for Will. She didn't know what she'd do if she found him, of course. Probably kiss him or attack him or both, if history served as any sort of lesson. For better or worse, though, he wasn't around, and she was able to get in an energizing five-miler uninterrupted.

After her run, she showered and headed for the dining hall, figuring she'd catch up with her roommate there. She was scanning the dining room tables when Kim came up behind her.

"Hey, teammate," he greeted her, tapping her on the shoulder affably. "Who are you looking for?"

"My better half," Gaia explained, frowning. "Have you seen Catherine? She was back in the room with me earlier, but I haven't seen her since I came back from my run. She never misses a meal. I swear, she's the only girl who can eat as much as I can."

Kim shrugged. "Sorry, nope." He grabbed his tray and followed Gaia to the long tables, scooting into a seat directly across from her. "You'll just have to make do with my company tonight."

Gaia smiled. "Lucky me," she said sincerely. "I actually did want to talk to you, anyway."

"Share," Kim prompted, cocking an eyebrow questioningly.

"I wanted to know . . . would you be willing to sit down with me to go over the details of the murder investigation? If I thought I was stressed before, when it was just one murder, I'm totally thrown now. I have a ton of notes and I was thinking, maybe it would help to have a fresh eye look them over. Crane says it's kosher as long as your input is purely anecdotal. I mean, I can't enter your opinion into the file or anything. And anything we discuss would be strictly confidential. But since you're the master profiler . . . well, it would really be a help," she finished.

"Of course," Kim said. "I just hope I have something useful to contribute."

"Trust me," Gaia said, "anything that you could contribute at all would be great. We're totally blocked. Unless Catherine's latest tech-whiz brainchild project pans out, we're up against a wall."

"No problem. How about later tonight?"

Gaia checked her watch quickly. "Well, Catherine and I were going to meet at the computer lab in an hour. I thought she was coming to dinner, but I assume she's there now. She probably just wanted to get a head start with her new program. How about we meet up around ten? Is that too late for you? I wanted to swing by the bookstore and pick up some supplementary materials. I think that'll be helpful for us by way of research."

"Ten it is," Kim confirmed. "It's not that late, and besides—I never get any sleep around here anyway. After a day of training

I'm exhausted, but my mind is going ten miles a minute. You know what I mean?"

"Trust me, I do," Gaia said. She knew all too well.

After all, lately when she closed her eyes at night, all she saw was Ann. Ann, Sam, Margaret, and Timmy. And that wasn't going to change until the murders were solved.

THE INCONSIDERATE TYPE

The temperature dropped dramatically once the sun went down at night, and Gaia found herself rubbing her hands over her upper arms as she made her way from the computer lab back to her dorm room. She was in a foul mood. In addition to not showing for dinner, Catherine had apparently decided to blow off their plans to meet up and go over the new search engine. Gaia hadn't pegged Catherine as the inconsiderate type, but she'd had to change her tune after waiting around impatiently for over an hour. She'd called first the dorm and then Catherine's cell, but there was no answer at either number. She assumed that the girl was holed up somewhere, working on the new program, too absorbed in it to focus on something as small and insignificant as the time. That really annoyed Gaia. She hated to be kept waiting, and she *really* hated when people assumed that their own time was more valuable than anyone else's.

She was mentally rehearsing her little speech to Catherine as she unlocked the door to their dorm room. So caught up was she in her righteous indignation that she almost didn't realize anything was different. But then it hit her: something was off.

The door, she realized. *It's unlocked. It's never unlocked unless one of us is home. And if Catherine were home, she would have answered her phone when I called.*

Tentatively she pushed open the door. And gasped.

The room was a disaster. Both desk chairs were overturned, drawers were open, and clothing was strewn everywhere. Who had done this? And why? The fact that Catherine was nowhere to be found made Gaia wonder if she'd been taken, along with— a quick scan confirmed—some of her things.

Gaia did a rushed inventory of her own belongings. Nothing was gone, though nothing was where it would normally be found, either. And it wouldn't have been too difficult for anyone who wanted to do it to upload half of her computer files onto a jump drive.

Gaia stepped back, reeling. Whether Catherine had left on her own or had been abducted, this situation was bad. Very bad. She shoved her hand into her pocket and grabbed her cell phone, punching in a series of numbers frantically. Right now there were only two people who could help her.

RESIDUAL AWKWARD TENSION

"And you say she didn't give you any indication that she was going anywhere?"

Agent Bishop stood in the center of Gaia and Catherine's room, surveying the damage, much as Gaia had a mere twenty minutes earlier. The moment Gaia had realized that their room had been ransacked, she'd called for backup. Bishop and Malloy had rushed right over, along with Crane and Hyde. No one knew what to make of the scene.

Gaia shook her head, dazed. "The last time we talked we agreed we were going to meet at the computer lab. She had some sort of program that she thought was going to be helpful in terms of cross-referencing the victims in our investigation." Now it didn't look like Catherine's program was going to get any play. It was a small concern, in light of Catherine's mysterious disappearance, but just one more issue that would remain unresolved for the time being. Just one more setback. How many more could they take?

"The room looked like this when you got back?" Malloy asked. His face was creased with worry. Any doubts that Gaia'd had that she might be overreacting to the situation had disappeared the moment Malloy had arrived. He didn't look like he was taking this situation lightly.

"Yes, I went to find Catherine at the computer lab," Gaia explained again. "But she wasn't there. I waited awhile, getting angry,"—she admitted, feeling guilty—"and then I came back to the room. The door was unlocked when I got here, which I thought was weird, because Catherine wasn't home. And when I pushed it open . . ." She gestured helplessly, indicating the mess she'd walked into.

Bishop exchanged a meaningful glance with her partner. "We're going to have to put out an APB," she said. "I just hope whoever has her . . ." She didn't bother to finish the grim thought.

"What's going on?"

Gaia looked up to see Will standing, freshly showered and looking concerned, in her doorway.

"I was on my way to the library when I heard someone talking in the halls, saying . . . Catherine is missing?" He surveyed the room. "My God—what happened?" He rushed inside and crossed to where Gaia sat, shell-shocked. "Are you okay?" Gaia nodded. "I have no idea what happened," she said, shrugging limply. "I came home and the room was a disaster. And Catherine is gone."

Will exhaled loudly. "Wow. Well, do you think it has to do with the case?"

"I don't know what to think," Gaia said shortly. She rested her elbows on her knees and pressed her forehead into her palms, frustrated.

"Maybe she was abducted because she saw the killer," Will suggested gently.

Gaia shook her head emphatically. "That doesn't make any sense. *I* saw the killer. I got a better look at him than she did. And that's not saying much. Why would someone take her and not me?"

"That's an excellent point," Malloy said, interrupting what had almost felt like a private conversation. "That's exactly why I can't have you investigating the case on your own anymore."

"What?" Gaia asked, panicked. "You can't take me off the case—not now! I'm the only one who's been involved since the beginning. I'm the only one who's seen the killer. Especially now that we don't know where Catherine is."

"Right. Which makes you a prime target," Will said. He

reached out and took her hand protectively, whatever residual awkward tension that remained from their last encounter taking a backseat to the newfound threat. "You can't investigate these crimes alone."

Gaia couldn't believe this was happening. Something horrible had happened to Catherine—her friend *and* her partner—and now she was being taken off her case? A case that meant everything to her? She took a deep breath and gathered her composure.

"I can get a new partner," Gaia said brusquely, her demeanor one of pure confidence and determination. "I can stay on the case if I have a new partner."

Malloy sighed wearily. "We can't take you off the case," he agreed. "You're deeper in it than anyone else."

"I can do it," Will volunteered eagerly. "I can take Catherine's place."

Gaia stared at Will in surprise. Given that they were usually at each other's throats, she couldn't believe that Will would volunteer to team up with her. Gaia knew that Will was going to be an incredible agent, but she couldn't help but worry that his competitive streak might undermine their ability to work as partners.

"Come on, Malloy, you know I can handle it," Will pressed.

Malloy nodded slowly. "You're right, Taylor. And actually, it works out pretty well since you two are paired for the practical applications course, too. This way you'll always be in close contact. You'll be able to keep an eye on each other just about all the time. That will be helpful—in case the killer *is* tracking Gaia—if the killer is the one who took Catherine."

Whatever concerns Gaia had about Will taking Catherine's place were erased for a moment as Will sat down next to her and took her hand in his own. A small shiver ran through her body and then suddenly she felt rather relaxed, as though being near him would somehow make everything okay.

She gazed at Will, but she was unnerved by the expression on his face. He looked pleased. A little too pleased, in fact. Gaia didn't like the feeling that was now ruining her brief sense of calm. What if he was using this tragedy as a chance to advance his career? He'd been jealous of Gaia's temporary badge right from the start. If this was his way of putting himself back in the game—and Gaia couldn't even believe this thought was crossing her mind—did that mean he could have had something to do with Catherine's disappearance? It seemed so ludicrous and impossible. Then again, the situation they were in seemed that way, too.

She couldn't dwell on this fleeting thought for much longer, though. Bishop and Malloy had called for backup, and the room would momentarily be crawling with specialists looking to run the whole place over with a fine-tooth comb: prints, photos, the whole nine yards. More than anything, Gaia wanted to help them, but she'd been told in no uncertain terms that it wasn't her responsibility. In this case, she was the friend of a victim. They'd question her further as they tried to find Catherine, but for now, all there was for her to do was step back and let the others do their jobs.

Will

A murder case. I'm working on a *murder case*. With Gaia.

This is going to be interesting. And maybe more than I bargained for. Working on a murder case is going to be intense and stressful, and working on it with Gaia? That will be confusing as all hell.

That girl—she's amazing. And no matter how hard I try, I just can't get a handle on her. She's smart—maybe even smarter than anyone I've ever met—but this is Quantico. This is the FBI. It's not like she's the first smart girl to ever walk through these doors.

She's athletic, of course—the only one who ever manages to beat me in any of our physical challenges. And I'm not going to lie; sure, I find it incredibly sexy, but it's infuriating, too.

Being around Gaia is like being on a roller coaster. Or worse, a Tilt-A-Whirl. One minute I'm on top and suddenly, before I can even blink, I'm down again. I've never had to work so hard to prove myself to someone, to prove myself in comparison to them. And it drives me nuts that the person I'm competing against is the person I'm most in awe of. It's a sick cycle.

If you want the real truth, it tears me up that I was put on this case as an also-ran, that I'm only working it now that Catherine's gone. I'm nobody's runner-up. And I'm going to prove that now.

Working with Gaia will be tricky. But it will also be good for me. On the one hand, it will force me to do my best. Because if anyone challenges me, it's Gaia Moore. Then there's the fact that being around her is inexplicably, indescribably all-consuming. And while I can't really foresee us reenacting our kiss scenario while working on the case, the slight chance that the possibility exists is more than enough to keep me going for a long while.

So yes, I realize that this is a murder case, and I appreciate the gravity of this situation, but nonetheless, I just have to say it again:

This should be interesting.

I want to be Gaia's partner, but I don't know that I'm capable of being equals. I want to be motivated by her, but I want to surpass her. And somewhere in the middle of all of this churning emotion, I want to kiss her.

I'm not sure how all of those things are going to fit together.

convincingly distressed

The sky was gray and overcast, threatening rain. Out in California, Gaia had come to take sunny skies and mild weather for granted, and so far, the weather in Quantico had mostly held out.

Perfect, Gaia thought. *What a nice day for a murder case.*

For once, she wasn't talking about Ann or Margaret's murder. The NATs were back in Hogan's Alley, as for their practical application course was known. It was, in effect, the site of a massive role-playing game. Hogan's Alley itself was an entire replica of a small town that had been built just beyond the proper training grounds on the base, and once there, the trainees were broken up into small groups, which were expected to solve highly realistic reenactments of cases together, the way agents would in the real world.

Gaia glanced at Kim and Will. They both stood, nervous, with their hands in their pockets. She guessed they probably didn't even realize that they were imitating each other's posture. *It feels wrong,* she thought. *It feels wrong without Catherine. To me and to them.*

Gaia missed her roommate, and she was damn worried about her, too. Gaia wasn't the only one feeling that way. Catherine's family and friends had been calling her nonstop, asking her if there was any news. Gaia didn't have the heart to turn them away, so she kept checking in with Bishop and Malloy to the point where she was becoming a nuisance. But Gaia didn't care—she sympathized with Catherine's loved ones, and she knew what it was like to feel helpless.

However, each time she approached her superiors, they told her that special agents were working around the clock on this case, but there was no new information. The anxiety was eating Gaia up inside. Mostly she'd become overwhelmed with the idea that Catherine had been harmed—or even killed. But once in a while, an errant thought would nag at her—the thought that this whole thing was a setup. What if Catherine had played Gaia and the rest of the NATs for chumps and was off somewhere sitting on a wealth of top-secret information?

Why would you assume that she'd do that? Gaia asked herself. *Just because you've been disappointed by so many other people in your life? That's not Catherine's fault. Friends trust each other,* Gaia reminded herself. After all, if Catherine had wanted to hack into the FBI's secure information systems, she probably could have done so without ever enlisting. She was that good.

In addition to worrying about Catherine, of course, Gaia acutely felt her absence. While the rest of the NATs were broken down into groups of four, Gaia, Will, and Kim would have to make do on their own. There was no such thing as "not fair" in the FBI.

Will jumped suddenly, then reached into his pants pocket and retrieved a cell phone. "Hello?" he asked brusquely. He listened intently for a minute, then clicked the phone shut again. "It's the next stage of the game," he said, essentially stating the obvious. "We have to report to the sheriff's office."

The trio made their way down "Main Street," trying not to pay any mind to the other trainees standing in clusters and barking into their own phones. The goal was to solve the crime before they did. A certain element of playing cool went into achieving this.

The sheriff was being played by an actor, Gaia knew, but at least he was being played by the same actor that he'd been played by before. He looked convincingly distressed on Gaia's team's arrival.

"There's been a bomb threat called in," he said simply. "The caller said it was a 'major public building.' But they didn't specify more than that."

Will stepped forward, forever the alpha male. "We'll find it," he assured the sheriff smoothly.

"My men are already out there with dogs," the sheriff said. "But you might be able to find the bomb before they do."

Gaia knew that was unlikely. The dogs were trained to sniff out explosives. Conversely, all she, Will, and Kim had to go on were their instincts, and, as Gaia was learning every day, instinct was way too imperfect a system when you were dealing with people's lives.

"Well, if it's a public space, I'm thinking it's either the town hall, the school, the post office, or the local diner—just because it's so heavily populated," Kim said, thinking aloud.

"We'll find it," Will repeated.

"You'd better get out there, then," the sheriff said gruffly. "The caller said it was set to detonate in thirty minutes."

It's not enough time. The thought played through Gaia's mind on auto-repeat as they walked from the sheriff's office and back down Main Street. Thirty minutes wasn't enough time to find—and defuse—a bomb. *Even if Catherine were here, we'd never make it.* She hated to be so negative, but the truth was that without Catherine, they were truly in trouble. She'd been the one who'd been able to stop the bomb so quickly during their class, right? It was particularly ironic, then, that she'd be missing now.

"So where do you think we start?" Kim asked, playing mediator.

"School?" Gaia suggested. "When you hear about bombs going off, it's always at a school."

"Not always," Will argued. Taking the opposite stance from Gaia was par for the course for him. "How often do you hear about bombs going off in municipal buildings or public spaces? Oklahoma City? The World Trade Center? I don't think the school is necessarily a sure thing."

"Fine," Gaia said, stopping in her tracks and placing her hands on her hips. "So how do you suggest we go about narrowing down our choices?"

Will smirked at her. "Well, I guess it's just a matter of trial and error," he said matter-of-factly.

"Great. I hope your trial takes you less than thirty minutes," Gaia snapped. "Not to mention your error." He was so smug. She wanted to reach out and . . . well, wipe that smile off his face.

The intensity of the thought surprised her. But then, most of her thoughts about Will were fairly intense.

"Guys," Kim said, physically stepping between them and raising his eyebrows, indicating his extreme displeasure at the turn this conversation was taking. "I have a thought as to how to get to the bottom of this."

Gaia and Will whirled to face Kim questioningly and he waved his arm in the direction of the post office. Masked, uniformed bomb squad members were jogging toward the various entrances, dogs barking maniacally and straining at their leashes.

"I'd say the post office might be a safe bet," Kim offered quietly.

"I'd say so," Will agreed, looking appropriately sheepish but not apologizing as such. "Any idea whether or not anyone else has noticed them?"

Gaia quickly looked to her left and then her right. "If they have, they're playing it really cool," she decided. "No one's come running, anyway. I think if we rush—and try to be subtle—we can get there first."

The group hastily quickened stride. As Gaia had suggested, they rushed to the post office and through the front door in time to hear a member of the squad yelling triumphantly. "Here it is!" he shouted. "I've got it!" They raced in the direction of the voice.

Great, Gaia thought. *Wires.*

The bomb was an exact replica of the ones they'd worked on in class, except that the wires were differently colored, which was problematic, since the color-coded wires were the part that

Gaia's photographic memory could recall to a T. A tangle of colored wires ran from the body of the bomb, coming to an angry nest of knots just at the base. It wasn't a complicated affair. If that photographic memory served, Catherine had managed to take it apart in, oh, about one minute flat. But Catherine wasn't here now.

Gaia ran up to it and crouched down, examining the makeshift machine without actually laying a finger on it. "I think it's the green wire," she said to no one in particular. "The one that we need to pull."

"You better hope you're right," the bomb squad worker who'd found it told her. "Otherwise we're in a whole lot of trouble."

"He's right, Gaia," Will said patiently, as if Gaia were either five years old, extremely slow, or both. It was plain to see he liked the idea of someone else getting on Gaia's case. "Why don't you let me take a crack at it?"

"What?" Gaia sputtered, nearly exploding herself from frustration and stress. *Relax,* she thought. *They're watching you. They're always watching, to see how you react when the pressure's on.* She took deep, even breaths and tried again. "What on earth makes you think you're any more qualified to look at this thing than I am?"

"Well, you couldn't deactivate it in class," he pointed out.

Gaia shot Will the look of death. "If I recall correctly, neither could you," she spat. "Catherine was the only one who could. But in case you forgot, she's not around."

"*Guys,*" Kim said insistently. "I know you're tense, but come on. Have either of you noticed how much time there is left on the bomb?"

Gaia and Will both whipped their heads back in the direction of the machine. Its digital readout blared *4:22*.

Oh, crap.

She knew that it wasn't real. That in four minutes and twenty-two seconds, if they weren't able to defuse the bomb, the only thing that would happen was that they would lose the latest installment of the game. And even if it *had* been a real bomb . . . Gaia wouldn't have been afraid. Gaia was never afraid. But the pressure was on, nonetheless, in the form of buckets of sweat pooling at the nape of her neck. "Four minutes!" she called to Kim, somewhat unnecessarily, given that he stood poised over her shoulder, fixated on the readout himself. "I can do this," she said, more to herself than anyone else. *I think.*

"You couldn't do it in class," Will repeated. "And I've been reading up on this stuff since then. You should let me try." He didn't sound ruffled or impatient, just calmly secure and confident.

Give it a rest, Will, Gaia wanted to shout. But she held her tongue. She had no idea which wire needed to be cut. If Will did, if he'd really been reading up on this stuff, then he was right—this was something he should handle.

But it killed her to step aside.

"Three minutes forty-nine," Will said insistently. "How about you make some room for me?"

Reluctantly she stood, glaring at Will. "Be my guest," she said snidely. Half of her fervently hoped he'd be able to dismantle the bomb—after all, they were playing for keeps here—and the other half didn't want him to have the satisfaction. She knew him well enough at this point to know that there would be *much* satisfaction. And probably gloating as well.

Will crouched down. He peered at the wires and very gingerly traced them with his fingertips. "It's not the green," he said, his voice so low it was practically a whisper. "You were wrong, Gaia." He murmured it, half mesmerized by his task. He wasn't gloating now, merely fixated. He pointed to the blue wire, indicating the space where it joined the base of the bomb. "This one," he said. "This is the one that sends the signals." Then, his movements suddenly as swift as they had just been tentative, he reached forward and grabbed at the wire. It snapped from the bomb.

All at once the clock on the bomb froze. Will let all of his breath out in one master sigh, letting his face collapse into his palms. Only then did Gaia realize how nervous he had been. *But he didn't choke,* she thought. She had to admit, as obnoxious as Will could sometimes be, he was going to make a damn fine agent one day.

"Good work, Agent . . ." the bomb squad officer said, stepping forward to shake Will's hand.

"Taylor," Will said, a grin of satisfaction spreading across his face. "Agent Will Taylor."

Suddenly a sharp horn sounded in the distance. That was it. This round of "the game" was over. Gaia, Will, and Kim each shook their heads and breathed deeply, hoping to shrug off some of the tension that the role playing had generated.

They wandered out back onto Main Street, shuffling along zombielike, trying to snap back into the real world. They could see the other NATs coming out from wherever they'd been investigating, doing the same thing.

Agents Bishop and Malloy strode into view purposefully.

Malloy marched directly over to Will and shook his hand. "Well done, Taylor. Another commendable round by your team—and even down a man. Impressive."

"Thanks," Will said, his "aw shucks" grin in full force.

"This young man, together with his teammates, managed to find and defuse the bomb in exactly twenty-six minutes," Malloy announced to the crowd of NATs looking on. "That's exactly one minute and fourteen seconds faster than the record set last year for this exercise. I hope you're all sufficiently impressed." The murmured whispers rising from the crowd suggested that indeed, they were.

Bishop stepped forward. "Consider this your introduction to the next phase of the game," she said. "That bomb may have been planted by a terrorist organization. Your job will be to determine if it was a singular crime or part of a larger plan. Of course, if it is a part of something larger, you're going to have to determine which organization is responsible and bring it down. Whoever planted the bomb may plan to strike again. They may succeed. As you've already learned, you're going to have to be on your feet constantly if you want your team to be the one to unmask them." She smiled. "That's it for now. You can return to your 'real' lives—keeping in mind, of course, that the game is never truly over."

Kim shrugged thoughtfully. "Terrorism. Or terrorist-like behavior. Interesting."

Will nodded. "Sure to be."

The boys continued their banter as they made their way across campus back to the dorms. Gaia held back from the conversation, though. She was tired. More than tired, she was deeply exhausted, all the way down to her very core. She was frustrated, too. She understood all too well the value of the lessons that she was learning at Quantico. But she was no closer to solving Ann and Margaret's murders than she'd been this time yesterday. And now her roommate was missing. Which was the priority? How could she possibly choose?

Answer: they both were. She had to deal with both and immediately.

It just seemed . . . it just seemed like there were bigger problems at hand than some imaginary game. But she knew that kind of thinking was dangerous. That kind of thinking was counterproductive. And awfully negative. Negative thinking was verboten to her these days. Wasn't it? She had vowed to herself after high school, when she'd hopped on a bus with little more than the sweatshirt on her back, that she was headed for a fresh start. Regardless of all of the amusement that fate had had at her expense, it was time to turn over a new leaf. Which meant embracing at least a certain level of positivity.

She couldn't help it, though. She wanted to be on board with the game. She desperately wanted to. But right now she had so much on her plate. Maybe too much. She hated to admit it, but dividing her energies was starting to feel like an impossible task. Gaia didn't know how she was going to juggle it all. Sooner or later something had to give, didn't it?

She just had to hope it would be later. Much, much later.

Gaia

Since I was little, my life has been dramatically different than that of anyone I've ever known. I've been the target of people who wanted to replicate my DNA, poked and prodded by doctors who wanted me to be a test subject for an antianxiety drug. I've been locked up in a loony bin and studied by mad scientists and hunted down in the street like an escaped convict.

Even my father, who meant the world to me, saw me as someone to be molded and shaped as he saw fit. He told me it was for my own good, and he was probably right. God knows those survival tactics sure came in handy. So to say that my existence has been unique would not be an overstatement.

I wanted to live a "normal life," but that wasn't an option. And so, somewhere along the line, I forgot how to be a regular person. Someone who understands group dynamics, for example. A team player. Wait—that's not even entirely true. I never forgot. To say I forgot suggests that at one point I *was* a team player. But how could I have been? I never had a team.

What I had was myself. My freakishly strong, Amazonian body. My intellect, or "inner resources," as my father likes to call them. The tools he passed on to me, and all before I'd even hit puberty. And so I went off on a vigilante justice spree. I was young and pissed as all hell. I thought I knew how to take care of myself and how to take care of others.

I thought wrong.

It only took a few hours to find out how wrong I was. During one interview Agent Malloy made certain to let me know what he thought of my self-imposed superhero complex. What I'd seen as survival tactics back in the day in New York City was actually big-time social maladjustment. And even after I managed to convince them to give me a chance, I still made some industrial-strength mistakes. Here I have a team. And I need to learn to play by the rules and trust those who are trying to help me.

At the same time, I have to fully participate in "the game," which just about kills me. My roommate is missing. I'm investigating a murder and I don't seem to be coming any closer to solving it. And the worst part of all of this is that the skill set I've come to rely on is suddenly, inarguably useless. I want to put the game aside for now and find the Lollipop Murderer. Actually, I can imagine what Malloy would say to that. He'd tell me to readjust my attitude. But to be honest, that's like asking me to readjust my personality—some things won't ever change.

Is Catherine's disappearance more important than a fake bomb in a fake town? In my heart I know the answer is a resounding yes. But it almost doesn't matter, because I'm no closer to finding her than I am to winning the latest challenge in Hogan's Alley. How can I move on to more important things that are happening in the real world when I'm too busy training in a pretend one?

Maybe there's a way to escape it just for a little while so I can tend to what really matters.

It's frustrating. Even with all that I've learned so far, I still can't stop the old Gaia from talking.

"Gaia, remind me again why you called us all here?" Will asked, collapsing into a chair in the main lounge of the library and groaning. "I was really hoping to hit the showers and maybe catch a nap before dinner. I haven't been sleeping at all this week."

"That's why God invented caffeine," Gaia said, brandishing her own oversized travel mug. "Step lively, partner. We need to talk. Kim—" she started, waving her cup in his general direction. "I wanted you here in a consulting capacity."

Kim smiled at Gaia, smoothing out the short-sleeve-over-long-sleeve double-T-shirt effect he seemed to have going on. "Gaia, darling," he said, raising one eyebrow questioningly, "have you been doing your homework again?"

Gaia flushed. "You could say that." She reached into her bag and pulled out stacks of copies and computer printouts, making very deliberate eye contact with Will. "I can't sleep, either," she told him. "So I decided to put the restlessness to good use."

"Characteristics of copycat crime patterns?" Will mused, reading aloud from the sheaf of papers that Gaia had passed to him.

"Here's the thing," Gaia said. "If we want to get to the bottom of the investigation, we need to figure out whether the murders are the work of a serial killer or a copycat criminal. Based on the research I've done, it's really too early to tell. But there's always the possibility that I'm missing something."

"Just a crazed, off-the-wall shot, huh?" Will asked.

Gaia ignored him. "Kim, I hope you don't mind, I know you're not technically working with us on this, but I think Will and I need an objective bystander, and the fact is that you probably knew all this"—she gestured again at her stacks of paper— "before you even got here. I already talked to Bishop and he okayed this, so you don't have to worry about breaching confidentiality or anything."

"You know I'm happy to help," Kim said, looking like he truly meant it.

"Here's the thing," Gaia said. "A copycat criminal is easy to pinpoint if you really go over the details of the crime. He's acting purely on rage and secretly longs for infamy. Unlike a serial killer, a copycat is really a show-off at heart and actually *wants* to get caught. So while a serial killer will do everything in his power to meticulously cover his tracks, a copycat will essentially always make one mistake—it's like his calling card."

"Serial killers usually do get sloppier, though, as time goes on," Kim pointed out. "They reenact the same scenario and become frustrated when they realize that they aren't reconciling any of their issues. Also, the need to possess the victim—as opposed to simply disposing of him or her in the most efficient way possible—overrides concerns about anonymity."

"True," Gaia admitted. She sighed. "It's not an exact science. And unfortunately, it seems we won't know for certain until there have been a few more murders to compare those to. Which is just not acceptable. Sitting back and waiting for more, I mean."

"Right," Kim agreed.

"So you're saying that if this is a copycat crime, basically there's some deviation between the first murder and the second that we're just not seeing?" Will asked, frowning.

"Exactly," Gaia said. "Now, I know you weren't actually at either of the scenes, but I've passed along copies of the reports that were filed at both."

Will quickly scanned the reports, holding them next to each other in his lap and literally shifting his head from side to side.

"Murder weapon, check, pattern of wounds, check, victim's background, check," Kim said, ticking off a mental list.

"The victim's backgrounds weren't exactly the same," Gaia interjected. "Ann was a waitress, Margaret was a housecleaner."

"For all intents and purposes, they're the same," Kim said. "Socioeconomic standing is often a more reliable variant than the specifics of their employment. *Unless . . .*"

"Unless what?" Gaia asked, trying to keep impatience from creeping into her voice.

"Well, unless there are several more murders, in which *all* of the victims share the same professional status. In which case one of these is a deviation, suggesting either a copycat or a major slipup on the part of the killer."

"Great," Gaia said, her shoulders slumping. "So you're telling me the only way to know if we're on to something is to sit back and wait to see if some other woman is sliced open? That's really proactive."

"It's not ideal, I know," Kim said sympathetically. "And hopefully if you keep on this case, some other means of solving it will present itself sooner rather than later."

Will suddenly sat up straight in his seat. "What about the lollipops?" he asked, jabbing his index finger at a point in the files.

"What do you mean?" Gaia asked.

"Well, Sam's was red. Timmy's was purple. That could be a deviation."

"Or it could be deliberate," Gaia shot back.

Will looked defensive. "Hey, you asked for our opinion. I'm just saying, that's something you could have missed is all."

Gaia bit her lip. "You're right." She checked her watch. "It's way too late to talk to Timmy or Sam tonight. But maybe we can swing by the foster care center tomorrow. We have Timmy's lollipop in evidence. We can bring it by Sam's and ask him to confirm that it's the same brand as the one he was given—even if it's not the same flavor."

"You think he'll remember?" Will asked dubiously. "He's a kid. He's going to panic and tell us what we want to hear."

"Maybe," Gaia said hotly. "But I don't see that we have another choice."

She was growing impatient, which was counterproductive. But before she had time to readjust her attitude, Kim's face took on a concerned expression. He reached into his pocket to fish out his cell phone.

"Agent Lau," he said expectantly. He paused for a moment, listening. Finally he snapped the phone shut again and looked at Will and Gaia.

"Hogan's Alley," he said tersely. "We're wanted. They've found something new."

FAKE NORMALCY

During the daytime Hogan's Alley was a utopian replica of small-town living. It was almost a sick joke that a place so suburban picture-perfect was actually the location of so many horrible crimes—even crimes of the imaginary variety. At night, though, the air of the prefab houses took on a sinister quality, giving way to a sense of fake normalcy and impending doom. Gaia wasn't pleased to find herself back in the sheriff's office, which was cold and all but deserted at this hour.

"Thank you for coming down here so late at night," the sheriff said, nodding at Kim.

"Not a problem," he replied. "What can we do for you?"
The sheriff held out a disk. "I'm not sure yet, but you can scan this and tell me what you find."

"Where's it from?" Will asked, stepping forward and plucking the disk out of the sheriff's hand. Gaia wondered if it bothered Kim to see Will assume the leadership position in the same way that it bothered her.

"Would you believe we found it inside the bomb you defused this afternoon?" the sheriff explained.

Gaia frowned. "Inside?" That was weird.

He nodded. "Yup. We took it apart after y'all left, and this was inside, just waiting for us."

"So someone wanted it destroyed," Gaia mused.

"Or they wanted us to find it," Will argued.

"Good point," Gaia said. She turned to the sheriff. "Thanks for calling us down."

"No problem," he replied. "Way I see it, since you were the ones that defused the bomb, you're the ones that this belongs to."

"We're going to have to take it back to one of the computer labs to read it," Gaia said. "We'll let you know tomorrow what we find."

The three of them thanked the sheriff again and headed back in the direction of the labs.

AUTHORITATIVE LILT

The trio trudged across the campus, feeling slightly defeated, though no one wanted to be the one to suggest as much aloud.

"You realize the irony of all of this," Kim said, giving voice to the thought that was plaguing them all. "With Catherine gone."

"I do," Gaia admitted, sighing. "We've got a real piece of evidence here. But it's a computer disk. And it's probably encrypted. Meanwhile, we're down one computer expert."

"It's fine," Will said, his voice taking on that authoritative lilt that he liked so much. "We can do this."

Surprisingly, Gaia appreciated his cocky attitude. Maybe Will's ego would give Gaia's psyche just the boost that it needed.

ENCOUNTERING DEATH

The next morning Gaia hunted down Malloy before breakfast. She found him in his office, hunched over a laptop, concentrating fiercely. "We need Catherine back," she said simply, "if we're going to win the Hogan's Alley game. None of us have the computer savvy that she has." She swallowed. "Besides, sir, I'm worried that you haven't got any new leads." *Am I being disrespectful?* she wondered fleetingly. She pushed the thought aside; concern for Catherine was far more pressing.

"Gaia," Malloy began. His tone was gentle. Gaia's skin instantly prickled. Malloy's tone was *never* gentle, and particularly not with her.

"What is it?" she demanded.

"We *do* have a new lead," he said. "You should sit down."

Gaia obliged warily.

"Catherine's laptop was found," Malloy said. "With some of her clothes, her wallet, and some toiletries—they were all in a duffel bag. The duffel bag was dirty and torn and showed signs of wear and tear. And it was all found on the side of the highway, just outside of Prince Edward County."

"Maybe Catherine was taken captive and she escaped," Gaia said.

"There was blood on the bag, Gaia, and on the road. It was tested, and it tested conclusive with Catherine's blood type."

"She could have been hurt and still escaped."

Malloy sighed. "Unlikely, due to the amount of blood." He looked at Gaia, his face a stony canvas. "The FBI believes her to be dead. We will maintain our postings of her as a missing person in the database, and her case will be open. But our pursuit will drop to a lower priority." He shook his head, looking as though he wanted to say more, but he didn't. Gaia wondered, looking at his expression, how much of this decision had actually been his own and how much had come from above his head. She couldn't ask, though.

"She can't be dead," Gaia said.

Even as the words left her mouth, she realized how hollow they sounded. *Why* couldn't Catherine be dead, after all? Maybe normal girls, girls with names like Suzie or Mary who lived in cute little houses with white picket fences, managed to get through the bulk of their lives without encountering death. But not Gaia. Her mother, her boyfriend, her closest female friend . . . Gaia knew people who had died. Too many people. It certainly wasn't unlikely that Catherine might be dead. Especially not if the FBI believed it to be true.

"I'm sorry, Gaia," Malloy continued. "I know this is a lot to digest. But we do have other things to discuss as well."

Gaia tried to push Catherine's death from her mind. "I know," Gaia replied. "The disk from Hogan's Alley. We ran it through the computer lab, but it's encrypted. None of the lab technicians know how to decode it."

"Never mind about that," Malloy said dismissively. "If you're serious about decrypting that code, you'll get someone else around here to help you. Someone from another team. But we need to find Taylor. I need to talk to you both."

Through the panic and confusion at the news about Catherine, it finally occurred to Gaia what Agent Malloy would have to discuss with her and Will. Her stomach clenched. In an instant she knew.

There'd been another murder.

"There's blood under her fingernails."

Will said it as a statement of fact, not a complaint or an issue that particularly bothered him. Rather he was methodically swabbing under the fingernails of the most recent victim and depositing the dried blood into glass vials. Gaia had to hand it to him—he was calm in a crisis. If this exam was as upsetting to him as it was to her, he wasn't letting it show one bit. He and Gaia had rushed over to the medical examiner's office to sit in on the autopsy.

"She was from Springfield," Ben said, consulting the file. "About five miles north of here."

"That's five miles farther than the first two murders," Will said. "Either the killer is broadening his scope or the copycats are."

"So this guy's taking his show on the road," Gaia speculated. "But he's still sticking to economically depressed areas, huh? This woman was . . . what?"

"Another waitress," Will said dully. "Another single mother."

Gaia sighed. "Great."

She watched as Will sorted the victim's clothing, preparing to send it to the lab for fiber analysis. She knew it wouldn't come back with any helpful information, though. It would come back reading that mainstream, commercial wool fibers had been found clinging to the victim's clothing. Meaning that she'd been attacked and killed by some freakish maniac wearing a big sweater. A big, dark sweater.

In other words, a big dead end.

Watching Will work, Gaia began to feel useless. If he could presume to participate in the ME's work, then so could she. She flicked on the glaring overhead light so that it beamed down on the body relentlessly. She didn't even flinch as she picked up Alice's digital camera. Photos of the body would have to be submitted to the lab so that the wound pattern could be analyzed. She knew without even running the report that it would be consistent with the first two—a Yukon Bay knife, stab wounds from a left-handed perp. If she thought about it for too long, it would start to feel like an exercise in futility. So Gaia decided not to think anymore. From now on, she was on autopilot. She was going to eat, sleep, and breathe this case. And she wasn't going to stop until she had solved it.

STALEMATE

Eating and breathing the case was one thing, but sleeping it, Gaia discovered, was a different matter entirely. Lying in bed that night, the only thing Gaia could see when she closed her eyes was the image of the third victim burned into the inside of her eyelids. Gaia knew that if she couldn't stop this killer soon, she'd never forgive herself. As it was, the guilt was tearing at her insides.

Was it really possible that she and Will weren't making any progress whatsoever? She'd done her homework; she'd tried to read between the lines. She'd interviewed any and everyone who seemed like they might be of help. Yet here they were, stuck in a stalemate while lives were at stake.

Sleep was impossible at this point. Gaia knew that if she did managed to drift off, all she would see would be the faces of the victims, the women she'd been unable to save. She groaned and pushed herself out of bed.

She padded to the bathroom, poured herself a glass of water from the tap, and settled back down at her desk. She opened up her laptop and with a few clicks of the mouse called up a blank Word document. The empty page was a beacon to her. Soundlessly, concentration so fixed, she was nearly entranced, Gaia began to type.

SICKLY YELLOW GLOW

The next morning Gaia was up and out before breakfast. She knew that the computer lab had staff on through the night, and she was hoping that they still had some life left in them. She patted her back jeans pocket, the one containing all of her requisite ID tags and something else. A zip disk. One that might, just possibly, offer some new insight into this case.

She pushed through the double doors of the lab eagerly, feeling the first glimmer of hope she'd felt in days. She found a very rumpled-looking technician sitting behind a desk, tapping away at a keyboard, the monitor bathing his face in a sickly yellow glow.

She slapped her zip disk onto the table in front of him.

"Can I help you?" he asked dryly, looking up from his work.

"Gaia Moore," Gaia said, reaching out to shake his hand. "Special Agent Gaia Moore."

"Lyle Perkins," the technician said, shaking her hand warily.

"Look, Lyle, I'm working on the Lollipop Murder Case," she explained. "If you run my ID, you can call up the details. I need your help."

"Well, sure," he said, sounding uncertain. "I mean, if I can."

"My partner was Catherine Sanders," Gaia explained. "If you pay any attention to the buzz around here, then you know that she disappeared. No one's been able to find her yet. But before she left, she told me about a program she created. Some sort of super–search engine with a mega-filter. She said that if we input all of the information we had about the different victims, the program could find any points of commonality between them, which would help us to narrow down the list of suspects."

The list of suspects was embarrassingly narrow as it was, now that Ned Riley had been released. Basically Gaia didn't have any suspects. Or rather, everyone that the victims had come in contact with was a suspect, but Gaia had no rationale for calling them in. Hopefully this would help.

Lyle looked up at her, wide-eyed. "I . . . I don't know," he admitted. "I mean, we've got search engines, of course—stronger ones than you think—but what you're describing . . . I'll be honest, I didn't really know it could be done. The larger the search engine, the more information it can access . . . but once you're pulling together that much information, you're sacrificing pinpoint accuracy."

"Come *on*," Gaia said, unable to keep her cool. Catherine

was a genius, sure, but was it possible that she was the only genius in the whole agency? How could that be? "You're the *FBI*. Please don't tell me that my ex-roommate is the only person in the world who knew how to work this program. Please." She sank down into a chair next to Lyle. "If you're telling me that, then I just don't know what I'm going to do. I am literally all out of ideas."

Something in her tone must have made Lyle take pity on her because his gaze softened, and he ran his fingers through his mad shock of thick, unruly curls. "Okay," he said, sighing. "Where's Catherine's computer?"

"It's in the evidence room," Gaia said slowly, realizing what Lyle had in mind. "I think I can bring it by as long as you wear gloves when you work on it. I'll talk to Malloy, make sure that it's been dusted. I think in this case he'll okay it."

"Well, if that's true, then why don't you bring the computer down to me after lunch?" Lyle offered. "Maybe if I have a look at it, I can work out the configuration of the program she was working on."

Relief flooded through Gaia's system like a drug injected straight into the bloodstream. Yes. That had to be it. That had to be how they'd get to the bottom of this. "Cool. I'll bring it down after lunch," she said. "You'll still be here?"

Lyle blushed. "I can come back."

"Thank you," Gaia said, her voice heavy with gratitude. "Thank you so much."

Gaia practically skipped to the evidence room after lunch. Bishop had given her the go-ahead, provided Lyle used gloves and extreme caution. The labs had already dusted for prints, though they hadn't picked up anything other than Catherine's. Her PowerBook was a super-sleek model, so it sure wasn't weighing Gaia down. She was feeling newfound levels of optimism about the case now that Lyle seemed to think there was a chance of cracking Catherine's computer program. Gaia didn't have any training until her hand-to-hand drill at three. That gave her plenty of time to hunker down with the geek patrol and figure out what was going on in the world of ones and zero—

Oh. Gaia had been so caught up in her enthusiasm that she hadn't been looking where she was going at all. And so, she had walked pretty much directly into a person. An attractive, well-built person.

Will person.

"Sorry!" she said breathlessly. "I wasn't watching where I was going."

"I can see that," Will said.

Gaia cautiously recoiled. Will's voice had a teasing tone to it, but there was an edge beneath the surface. "Something wrong?"

"Where *are* you going?" Will asked.

"I was just going to the computer lab," she explained. "I think I may have a lead on . . ." She trailed off, realizing exactly what was bothering Will. "I was just going to have one of the technicians look over Catherine's computer. She'd been working on a program that would cross-reference the murder victims through a super-filter. It would really give us a leg up in terms of leads. I came by your room, but you weren't around."

It was hard for Gaia to be deferential in the face of Will's jealousy. She knew that as Will's partner, part of her job was to work "with" him, which meant, at times, accommodating his quirks and personality tics. Not to mention, she was also his friend—and maybe more. But how was she supposed to work *with* someone who was basically against her success?

"Obviously I don't have a problem with you making progress on the case," Will said. "But I do have a problem with you constantly going behind my back. How am I supposed to help if you aren't being level with me?"

Frustrated, Gaia felt her temper soar. She was frazzled and stressed and tired of walking on eggshells around Will. This investigation had started as *her* show. She'd been put on it specifically because she'd been the one to sense something fishy and locate the first body, she'd seen the perp, and she'd been the one thinking about the case day in and day out, ever since she'd found Ann ripped wide open on her living room floor. But what good was her having seen the perp? What could she really identify about him after all? And in the meantime she'd lost a roommate, and she still had to contend with the not insignificant challenges of coping with the NAT training schedule. Whether or not Will was her boyfriend—and the evidence was increasingly mounting that perhaps, in fact, he was not—she needed his support.

"Listen," she said, as patiently as she could, "I wasn't trying to go around you. I was *working*. I was up all night turning the case over in my mind, trying to figure out how to get us out of this rut we've fallen into. Because in case you haven't noticed, we're pretty much out of luck when it comes to suspects, motives, or clues. So maybe I was a little focused, you're right. Maybe if I'd been thinking clearly—if I'd been able to get, oh, I don't know, three consecutive minutes of sleep last night instead of sitting at my computer, running on basically caffeine and fumes, maybe it would have occurred to me to try more than once to find you. To bring you with me. As it was, I was a little out of it. And I probably assumed I'd just run into you later. Since we're partners and all."

"Right," Will said. "You were tired, you were focused, so you figured you'd just sidestep the standard procedure. Gaia, that tactic hasn't exactly worked out so well for you up till now, has it?"

Low blow, Will Taylor, Gaia thought, so upset that she couldn't even look at him. And what really burned her up was that he was right. She was going to have to get it together if this was going to work. There *was* such a thing as standard operating procedure here. It was all *about* SOP. If she had any insights on her case, she had to tell her partner about them, not just assume that she'd run into him on his way out of the computer . . .

Hey. Wait.

On his *way out of the computer lab?*

Gaia paused, willing the gears in her mind to come to a halt. "What are *you* doing here, if I may ask?" she demanded, her voice low.

Will looked away. "I was at one of the labs," he said.

"Doing what?" she pressed. "And why do I have a feeling this is going to be good?"

Will nodded shortly. He refused to make eye contact. "Look, I was . . . I managed to decode the disk from Hogan's Alley."

Gaia's eyes flew open. This was great news, but under the circumstances, she could hardly appreciate it. "By yourself?" she asked slowly. "Without the rest of your team?"

Will didn't bother to answer her, but his silence was damning enough. "The disk contains the origins of the bomb," he said. "But I still don't know which organization is behind it. We're going to have to do some research."

"We," Gaia repeated, incredulous. "Yes, I guess we are. We'll just have to meet up and do it together. You can bring us up to speed. That's what teammates are for, right?" She glared at him. "It's a good thing you're so up on your SOP."

With that, she shot him one last look of disgust and pushed right past him into the computer lab. In her opinion, there wasn't anything left to say.

Gaia

Trust. It's an interesting concept. Basically, my own sense of trust was just about completely shattered when my mother was killed by her own brother-in-law. As horrifying as that was to me, I assumed I had hit rock bottom.

I was wrong, of course. My father then skipped town for reasons that are still not entirely clear to me. He claims to have been protecting me, and I'm sure he feels that he was. But it doesn't change the fact that I was shunted from foster home to foster home, constantly under the guardianship of people who just didn't have my best interests at heart.

Yes, I have some trust issues.

The thing about this place, though, is that whatever my weird-ass neuroses are, I'm going to have to let them go if I want to make it here. I'm going to have to learn to let people in. Certainly I'm going to have to learn to be straight with my teammates and partners. This is life and death here—and that's no exaggeration. If we can't rely on each other, then we really don't have anything. I get that now. I really do.

The question is, does Will?

With all of his testosterone-fueled posturing, after all of his flirtations, his arrogance—the kisses, the sparring, the hot-and-cold behavior—he's finally managed to genuinely piss me off. He's giving me a hard time about circumventing procedure and meanwhile he's cutting corners himself? No way.

The boundaries of trust have been violated, and I don't know how to rebuild them. I had thought my relationship with Will was complicated. I had thought he was an enigma. But at the very least, I always assumed he was trustworthy. Now I'm thinking maybe I had it wrong.

If that's the case, then we really are up the creek. And maybe Will has a paddle. But in light of recent events, can I really expect him to share?

letting him out of her sight

"Okay, what's our agenda here?" Gaia asked, being deliberately businesslike as she and Will stood outside the computer lab again. This time things were different, at least in that they had come to the lab together. But the air between them was still charged with tension.

Will rolled his eyes. "I'm going off to play with the Hogan's Alley disk. I'm hoping that some of the coding will be indicative of its source. You, on the other hand, are going to deal with Catherine's computer. Hopefully you'll be able to trace that filter program she was working on." He smirked at her. "I'm dealing with the game, and you're dealing with the case. We're the model of efficiency."

Gaia sighed and watched Will storm through the doors and stalk off to his own terminal. He was right—working separately was the most efficient course of action. But considering the tenor of their recent conversations, she didn't like the idea of letting him out of her sight. Whether that was because she admired him, didn't trust him, or both was unclear. And highly disturbing.

Very healthy, Gaia, she thought.

She followed Will inside and presented the laptop to Lyle as though it were a shiny birthday present. Fortunately, his eyes lit up at the sight of it. "Great," he said. He pulled out a seat for

Gaia right next to his own. "Settle in." He snapped on a pair of latex gloves and laid the computer down on a special mat.

Gaia sat down next to him, plunking a large cup of coffee onto the desk next to the computer. Lyle looked at her like she had three heads. She hastily moved the cup a few inches to the right.

A few quick taps on the keyboard and suddenly he was in the computer mainframe, spare, spindly letters of code running across the screen in early Atari–style font. Gaia was reasonably well versed in computer science, but this? This was just nonsense.

"What are you doing now?" she asked, pulling her hair out of her face and leaning in.

"Look," he said, jabbing a skinny index finger at the screen. "Those are the program files on Catherine's computer. It all looks pretty normal, though. I don't see anything advanced, like the one that you describe. Unless . . ." He trailed off, using the arrow keys to move up the screen as though he were climbing a ladder. "This file is compressed. Let's see what we have here." He hit one of the control functions.

Suddenly the entire screen shifted. Black gave way to vivid blue, and numbers began running up and down in vertical columns.

"Whoa," Lyle said. "Okay, that's weird."

"But it could be something, right?" Gaia asked, biting her lip nervously.

"It could definitely be something," Lyle said. "Yup, that's something."

The columns blinked once and evaporated, leaving behind a list.

Gaia stared at the screen, uncomprehending. "What's *that*?" she asked. It looked like a list of addresses and post office boxes.

POB 542 Benghazi, Libya
POB 631 Urus-Martan, Chechnya
POB 3321 Abu Dhabi, United Arab Emirates

"Um, wait. What's that?" Gaia repeated dully, a cold finger of dread creeping its way up her spine.

"Not sure," Lyle murmured. He leaned from Catherine's screen back over to his own terminal. He opened up one of his secure databases and punched in a few numbers. "It looks like . . . it looks like a list of . . . terrorist sleeper cells?" He sounded incredulous, like either he didn't believe it or didn't *want* to believe it.

Then Lyle's brow furrowed in worry. "There's something else here."

"What?" Gaia asked, snapping back to attention and leaning in once again.

He pointed at the screen again. "Do you see that? That's a log of the last few times that someone has accessed this program."

"But . . . but that was just yesterday," Gaia said, not understanding. "Catherine's been gone for days."

"According to Malloy, Catherine's *dead*," Will pointed out quietly, coming up from his post at his own monitor to peer over Gaia's shoulder.

"Yes, well, according to this log, the program was accessed remotely yesterday," Lyle explained. "Meaning that Catherine could have used it regardless of her location."

"But not if she was *dead*," Will repeated.

"But that—" Gaia started. *That doesn't make any sense,* she thought. "Could someone else be using her computer remotely? Whoever killed her?"

Will stepped forward and cleared his throat. "Can you trace the access?" he asked.

Lyle coughed nervously, his eyes darting around the room as though he were afraid the computer was somehow tracing *them*. He looked at Will.

"I can try."

ANYTHING TO DO WITH GAIA

"Sleeper cells?"

Malloy looked at Gaia and Will with concern. "Someone has been accessing terrorist sleeper cells remotely from Catherine's computer?"

Gaia nodded. "That's what it looks like, sir. PO boxes that don't check out. Not through any of our databases. I can't think of another reason why a remote cell would be so deep under the radar."

"Good work, you two," he said, smiling tightly at them from behind his desk. "You can leave the computer with me. I'll need to brief Agent Bishop on the recent findings."

Gaia fidgeted in her seat. "I want to help," she said.

Malloy looked at her questioningly. "I'm assuming you mean that you want to help locate whoever killed Catherine?"

Gaia nodded. "Sir, it's something I need to do."

"Gaia," Bishop said, "your findings so far have been invaluable, definitely. But you've got a serial killer to investigate in addition to your regular duties as a trainee. Not to mention you're way too close to this case. I can't allow it."

Gaia saw that there was no point in arguing. Malloy meant what he said. Catherine's case might still be open, but it didn't have anything to do with Gaia anymore.

QUITE A BIT OF EXPERIENCE

They weren't more than three paces outside of Bishop and Malloy's offices before Will grabbed Gaia by the elbow.

"Are you insane?" he hissed.

"No. But maybe you are," she replied, indicating his fist closed around her forearm.

Dutifully he dropped her arm, contrite. "I'm sorry. It's just . . . this is dangerous, Gaia! You need to let Malloy and Bishop do their jobs and trust them if they're telling you that you're in over your head."

"Will, this is the FBI. In case you hadn't noticed, we're training for dangerous situations. We're supposed to be learning how to handle them."

"Gaia, come on. You know the score. I'm not trying to put you down. But this *is* the FBI. They're not as well equipped to handle a foreign threat as the CIA is. Which means you may not have the backup that you need to go after Catherine."

She paused. Unfortunately, Will was right—and this was something she'd had quite a bit of experience with.

Seeing her hesitation, Will continued. "This is too dangerous for a NAT. You know it as well as I do. You don't know what you're getting yourself into. Look, Gaia," he said, dropping his voice an octave and stepping closer to her, "I know things have been . . . ah . . . awkward between us. There's something going on. You feel it, I feel it, but neither of us knows what to do with it. Maybe it's time we dealt with our feelings?"

Gaia shrugged noncommittally. "Maybe."

"I'll be straight with you. I don't want you to investigate Catherine's disappearance, because I care about you. Because I *worry* about you. I wouldn't want anything to happen to you."

Gaia's cheeks blazed. This sudden surge of affection was the last thing she'd expected from Will. It had been literally years since she had allowed herself to have feelings for a guy. But she had to admit that like it or not, the feelings were there now. Complicated, bogged down by confusion, yes. But there nonetheless. "I . . . I care about you, too," she said, struggling with the complicated flux of emotions she was experiencing. She appreciated his concern—more, probably, than she was willing to admit. But something in her, deep down, knew that she couldn't just sit back and let others work Catherine's case. Catherine was her friend. She had to get involved.

She looked up to find Will gazing at her with newfound tenderness. How to tell him that she wasn't ready to step aside on Catherine's case? He'd be devastated. Especially since she knew how hard it must have been for him to confront his romantic feelings for her. "I'll think about it," she said finally. It wasn't quite a lie.

"Great," Will said, obviously relieved. He grabbed her hand. "One more thing?"

Gaia was floored. Will actually looked shy and nervous. What the hell was going on here?

"Have dinner with me tonight. You need the distraction—just for an hour. We'll find the closest thing this town has to a romantic restaurant. Besides, we're due for a celebration, aren't we? Getting praise from Malloy is like getting blood from a stone."

Gaia had to laugh. "You're right," she admitted. "But I'm not sure it's such a good idea for us to get involved while we're partners."

"Gaia," Will said gently. "We're already involved." He had a point, she knew. Like it or not—*convenient* or not— they had feelings for each other. And whether or not they decided to pursue a real relationship, they needed to deal with their feelings. Otherwise their work would suffer—along with everything else. This wasn't quite a reconciliation. They still had a long way to go toward figuring out their relationship— romantic or otherwise. But it was a step in the right direction. An effort to mend fences.

"Okay," she said, giving in to the moment and allowing herself a small grin. "I've got a few things to do, so maybe we could meet up somewhere."

Will smiled back. "I know the perfect place. Lombardi's. It's this family-style joint just off of the interstate. Ever been there?"

Gaia shook her head. "Nope, but it sounds good. I'm incredibly pro-carbs."

"Great, then you won't be disappointed. I'll call you later with directions. Does seven work for you?"

The word *disappointed* kept repeating itself over and over again in Gaia's brain, as if it were an echo in a cave.

"Yes, seven is perfect," she said over the pounding of her heartbeat. "Can't wait."

Will

I'm finally going out with Gaia Moore—on a real, honest-to-goodness date, where kissing will be appropriate for once. She's nothing like any of the girls I know from back home. Now that I think about it, most of my ex-girlfriends really gave in to me. They kind of did whatever I wanted or needed or what I thought was best for them, without much arguing or resistance. And eventually, the relationship would bore me.

Perhaps that explains why I can't back away from Gaia. She's the only person who has ever challenged me. Everyone else just accepted me at face value, but with her, I have to dig deep and prove myself, which is exactly what I've been doing this whole time at Quantico—proving that I'm the best agent in my class.

It's funny, though. Being with Gaia makes me doubt that I'm the best, and not just because she's so unbelievably good at everything that she does. I question my abilities mostly because when Gaia is faced with a tough situation, she *never* wavers. I know I'm stubborn to a fault, but what she has inside of her—it doesn't seem to be stubbornness at all. It's like this impenetrable force that keeps pushing her forward, regardless of the danger or the consequences that are ahead of her.

That's why I'm relieved that she agreed to think twice about investigating Catherine's murder. Not only would she get into a lot of trouble and put everything that she's worked for at risk, but she could get hurt . . . or killed.

God, I can't even bear to think of something like that happening. And I know what that means—I've let her into my heart.

I just hope she doesn't break it.

Will had a feeling that Lombardi's might be a far cry from the quaint Italian restaurants that Gaia had known back in New York City. Rather than a charming, out-of-the-way spot located on a quiet block in Little Italy, Lombardi's was one of the more romantic places to be found in the immediate vicinity of the training base, which made it a great place for their first date.

True to his word, Will had called Gaia earlier to give her directions to the restaurant, but she hadn't picked up her cell phone, so he'd just left all the details on her voice mail. Now it was seven on the dot, and Will was sitting at the restaurant bar, looking freshly scrubbed and clean in a pair of olive chinos and a polo shirt. He was also uncharacteristically nervous—to the point where he was conscious of how much he was sweating. He kept sipping on his bottle of imported beer and picking at the label, hoping that Gaia would show up before he started tearing out his hair or something.

However, Will's anxiety was growing. He gazed at his watch about twelve times before placing another call to Gaia. It was unlike her to be a half hour late, and if it was one thing Will had mastered at Quantico, it was the art of suspicion.

Fifteen minutes later, another one of Will's calls rang through to Gaia's voice mail again. He grunted in frustration and shoved his phone into his pocket. Where the hell was she? He was too upset to really admit to himself that he probably already knew.

Just then the host came by to check on him. "Sir, do you want me to seat you at a table while you wait for your friend?"

Will thought about it for a second, and then shook his head. "No, thanks. My friend won't be joining me tonight."

He ordered another drink. When a fourth pint was placed in front of Will, he gave the bartender a big tip, knowing that for the next couple hours this guy going to hear a lot of sob stories about the girl who got away and the stand-up guy who got stood up.

Gaia

I've left so many things behind in my life, but I never thought that abandoning Will would be this hard. Sure, I had an inkling that I might feel guilty, but I'll be damned—I actually feel . . . sad that I'm not with him right now.

But I can't give into those emotions. I have to keep my eyes on the road and my mind on what's important. Something terrible has happened to Catherine and I have to help her. I must do this because no one else will. I'm not going to stand idly by and watch the FBI sweep Catherine under the rug and pretend that she didn't even exist. Even if she is dead, doesn't she deserve the respect of being brought home to those who love her? I think that if Will were here with me, he'd agree that Catherine should be treated with honor.

But he's not even close to being here. He's gone from waiting for me to giving up on me, I'm pretty sure of that. Although we've had our differences, I've always known Will believed in me. No matter how much he tried to hide it, I could see a special gleam somewhere in his eyes. When I come back to Quantico—that is, if I come back still breathing—what will I see in his eyes then? I don't even want to imagine.

I know he's going to be angry and disappointed. But he'll be in good company—joining the ranks of the many people I've let down, including myself.

I can't afford to disappoint Catherine, though. She's out there, I know she is. It's only a matter of time before I find her, and when I do, Will might understand why I had to leave without saying goodbye.

If he doesn't, I'll have to deal with it the only way I know how: by accepting the things I can't change and forcing myself to move on . . . .

Here's a sneak peek at the latest book in the thrilling new series

FEARLESS® FBI
AGENT OUT

Gaia

Transcribed Digital Audio Log
Agent Gaia Moore recording
FBI Case #KB2344—Sanders, C.
cc: Agent Pelton—Homeland Security
CLASSIFIED—Code 22V

Date and Time Stamp of Original Recording:
August 21, 2:34 a.m.

Gaia Moore: It's 2:30 a.m. Agent Gaia Moore recording. I can't give a case number, because this case does not exist—not as far as the FBI is concerned. They think Catherine is already dead. Apparently they're prepared to let her name just fade away on some inactive missing-persons list for the next twenty years without lifting another finger, but with all due respect to you, Agent Malloy, I think that's a crock. You have no idea what's happened to Catherine, and neither do I. One abandoned laptop and some blood on a lost duffel bag don't tell you anything. You can't just declare her dead and be done with it—she deserves more than that. Catherine and I have pulled each other through every single day of training. She never once lost faith in me, and I am not about to lose faith in her. She is more than my friend; she's my *partner*, and I doubt very much, sir, that you could write your partner off as easily as the bureau has written off Agent Sanders. I think that's lousy police work—lazy and shortsighted—and I think I can do better. I'm stating that for the record here, in the hopes that you and the rest of the bureau will understand my motives.

Eventually you're all going to see why I had to do it this way—sneaking off base in the middle of the night to find her. I admit I feel a little foolish. I feel like I'm seventeen years old again—sneaking out on my foster parents to dodge some ridiculous curfew. I swore to myself that I'd never be a rebellious teenage cliché again, but there you have it: I am what I am. I know how unprofessional this is, believe me. I would have loved nothing more than to have pursued this investigation *with* your permission, sir; you just weren't inclined to offer it.

You've probably already declared me AWOL. Someone must have noticed that I'm not in my bed and I'm nowhere to be found on the whole Quantico base. I wouldn't be surprised if you'd already started proceedings for my termination, but all I can say is . . . I'm doing what I think is right. I'm doing what I need to do. If you knew more about my past, you'd understand. [*Pause.*] What am I saying? You're the FBI—you probably know *everything* about my past. So maybe someone on some disciplinary committee who hears this recording will consider my history and show me some mercy. Maybe *you'll* understand, Malloy. . . . I'm just not going to write off another friend. I can't. And I don't see the point of having this badge or this gun if I can't even help my own partner. I don't care how hopeless you all think it is. I couldn't care less. [*Recorder off.*]

[Recorder On—Time Stamp—2:48 a.m.]
I don't know why my foot is still on the gas. I don't even know why I'm going in this direction. My eyes keep drifting out the driver's-side window—looking for signs of her body in the gravel on the side of the highway. That's what I've been reduced to here. I know it's irrational and naive, and I should

be ashamed to call myself FBI, but that's what I'm doing. A dog would have a better chance of finding her like this. I need more to go on. I need *something* to go on. Jesus, I feel like such an amateur, talking into this thing. You trained me to take audio notes in an investigation, so that's what I'm doing. You said it would keep my thoughts organized. You said it would help me flush out the right clues. Like this recorder is going to help me find her out here in the dark on this completely abandoned highway. I don't think so. I don't even need a machine to help me keep track of clues. I don't forget things. Ever. You can call it a photographic memory, but it's more complicated than that. You might have noticed, Agent Malloy . . . I'm not like the other trainees. [*Pause.*] Note to self: erase that last part.

The point is, I'm not really using this recorder to take notes on this case. I'm using this recorder because it's the only partner I've got right now. I need someone to talk to while I look for her . . . even if that someone is me. I'm alone out here. And I mean that in every sense of the word. [*Pause.*]

A message for Will . . . Will, I'm sorry. I'm sorry I stood you up for dinner—that was just lame. But more than that, I'm sorry if you think I don't listen enough. I know you didn't want to me to do this, but . . . Look, most of all I'm sorry for leaving the Lollipop Murder Case right in the middle of the investigation. I'm sorry for leaving it all in your hands. I hope Malloy doesn't come down on you too hard. I hope you don't feel like I've abandoned you or abandoned the case or the victims or anything like that. We *will* solve that case, Will. We'll find the killer, I'm *sure* of it. Just give me a little time. If you can carry the case for just a few days . . . I'll be back. I swear I will. And I'll bring Catherine with me.

Absolute Nowhere, USA

The sun had risen, but Gaia hardly noticed. Somewhere along the way, the sky had shifted from moonlit black to ugly amber to its current shade of ash white. How long had she been driving now? The miles of gas stations and convenience stores had all melted into one big peripheral blur. Her eyes stung like hell from exhaustion, and the harsh glare of the late morning haze was only making it worse. She could practically hear her body pleading for an hour of sleep, but rest was out of the question. All that mattered now were the worn-out street signs overhead.

She hunched further over the steering wheel, squinting up through the dusty windshield of Catherine's Nissan Altima to decipher the faded names. Palmer Street . . . Mortimer Street . . . Winslow Road . . . but no Cherry Lane.

Where the hell is 1309 Cherry Lane?

The unfamiliar address had been rattling in her brain for three hours now—ever since Lyle had whispered it nervously to her over the phone. She could still hear his nasal voice cracking with anxiety. . . .

"I shouldn't be doing this, Gaia. You know I shouldn't be doing this. Malloy was just in here asking questions. He's pissed, Gaia. You know you're in serious—"

"I know that, Lyle. I know. The trace. Could you trace the origin of the signal or not?"

"Hold on."

"Lyle, do not *put me on hold!"*

"Just hold on, *okay? I have to check the doors. They're search-*
ing the whole complex for you, you know."

She knew she'd put Lyle in an unfair position. After all, he was
just a spindly little FBI lab tech—it wasn't like she wanted to
make him an accomplice to her unauthorized investigation. But
around seven in the morning, somewhere in the middle of
Richmond, Gaia had come to terms with reality. Her *only* legitimate lead was back at that computer lab in Quantico. There'd
been no other choice but to call Lyle on his personal cell and pray
he'd already reported to the lab—which, thank God, he had.

All she had going for her was that cryptic computer program
Catherine had left behind. Gaia had found the program still running
on Catherine's computer after she'd disappeared. Gaia had assumed
it was the high-powered search engine Catherine had been boasting
about—a little piece of software she'd created that was supposed to
cross-reference all the evidence in the Lollipop Murder Case and
spit back potential suspects. But once they'd examined her computer more closely, they'd realized that Catherine's program was
collecting a *very different* kind of information. Her turbocharged
search engine had found something that it had clearly not been
meant to find—namely, an index of Latin American addresses that
looked an awful lot like addresses of terrorist sleeper cells.

This bizarre discovery had left Gaia and Will in a near-
catatonic state of puzzlement. But that was just the beginning of
the strangeness. Not only was Catherine's program gathering this
explosive information, but someone, it seemed, was *still* accessing the information in her absence. According to Lyle, even

though Catherine had disappeared days before, someone had been using her program as recently as twenty-four hours ago.

Could that someone be Catherine? Could she be out there somewhere trying to access her own computer? Could someone be forcing her to access it? Or what if it was someone else entirely? Some nameless, faceless asshole who'd already gotten rid of Catherine and was trying to nab the information for himself? These questions were the only thing keeping Gaia's eyes glued open and focused on the road ahead.

Will had asked Lyle if there was any way to trace the access. Lyle said he would try, but trying wasn't good enough. Gaia knew she'd have to push Lyle to get the info she needed—even if it meant taking advantage of his rather obvious crush on her. So with just the right combination of dominance and flirtation, she'd finally managed to coax poor Lyle past his initial anxiety until he'd coughed up an address.

"Baltimore, okay? The program was accessed from a telephone modem in Baltimore. The Verizon map pinpoints the signal at Cherry Lane near Ditmar Street. The exact address is 1309 Cherry Lane. Someone in that house logged on to Catherine's computer in the last twenty-four hours."

"You're a genius, Lyle. You seriously are a goddamn genius. I don't know how to thank you for this."

"Well, maybe when you get back, we could go out for some—"

"I've got to go, Lyle. We never had this conversation, okay?"

"You're damn right, we never had this conversation. I could be fired just for talking to—"

Click.

And so here she was, searching in vain for Cherry Lane. She

would have asked Lyle to map out a route for her, but she knew she'd kept him on the phone too long as it was. Another thirty seconds and the bureau would have been tracing Lyle's call, personal cell or not—and she would not risk getting him into any more trouble. She'd have to find Cherry Lane the old-fashioned way.

Once she'd made it into Baltimore, she asked for directions at a gas station, but the "attendant" with the faded faux-Nike Just Do Her T-shirt hadn't been much help. She'd only been able to make out every other word he said. All she'd learned was that Cherry Lane was a few miles south and a number of blocks west. But the other half of his unintelligible directions was a seemingly endless repetition of the words *left, right, old church,* and *Old McDonald's,* which Gaia was reasonably sure was not an old man's farm, but rather the term this man used to describe his favorite dining establishment. Eventually she did find her way to Ditmar Street, but Ditmar seemed to go on forever. . . .

"Jesus," she breathed through nearly closed lips, surveying the row of crumbling houses up ahead. There was no denying it: America could be one ugly-ass eyesore of a country. It seemed the city council had taken a meeting and decided to give up altogether on the outskirts of Baltimore. Each little house looked more forgotten than the last, from the broken, soot-covered windows to the rusted-out aluminum siding, to the tattered Stars and Stripes hanging tenuously over the piles of bricks that stood in for porch steps. This sure as hell wasn't the lush backwoods of Quantico, Virginia. It wasn't the pristine sunny streets of California or even the rich historical filth of New York City. No, this was something else entirely.

This was Absolute Nowhere, USA. Suburban degradation in all its glory.

Please don't let her be in one of these houses, Gaia thought, slowing the car to cruising speed. *Maybe Lyle has no idea what he's talking about.*

She was so distracted by the urban sprawl that she nearly passed right by the magic words. She quickly slammed on the brakes and backed up a few yards. All her exhaustion drained away once she saw the faded white letters on the rusty blue sign overhead:

Cherry Lane.

It's about freaking time, she thought, slamming her foot down on the gas. The tires skidded with a deafening screech as she turned the sharp corner and picked up the pace, eyeing every numbered address that hadn't fallen off its facade. And finally her marathon drive came to an end. The nine might have slipped its hinge to become a six, but the rotting house before her was most definitely none other than 1309.

She pulled over to the side of the road and turned off the transmission. The engine sputtered with a long sigh—she could almost feel the Altima thanking her for the much-needed rest.

She sat there for a moment in silence, examining the house from inside the car. Just as expected, it was not a pretty sight. The warped, hospital-blue siding gave the house an eerie generic flavor, as though it didn't want to be noticed. The porch door was boarded up with a thick slab of wood and couched in too much shadow to be seen clearly. The rest of the porch was bare, with the exception of a filthy black barbecue grill that a family of spiders had long since made their home. There was no front lawn to speak of—just a makeshift little garbage collection on a patch of black dirt. Anyone with a conventional genetic code would have taken one look at this place, locked all the car doors, and called for backup. But Gaia's genes were far from conventional. She could already feel a hungry buzz in her chest where the fear should have been. She was aching to kick through that knotty plank-of-wood door, but she thought better of it. She'd learned her lesson about rash behavior at Quantico, and she had no intention of repeating her mistakes.

Gaia might have gone AWOL, but that was the *only* thing about this investigation that would not be squeaky clean. Authorized or not, she was going to conduct this search like the professional she was. She would bring Catherine back, and she'd do it by the book, and Malloy and the rest of them would have nothing left to say but "Thank you" and "You have our deepest apologies for underestimating you both." She had already acquired a wealth of knowledge at Quantico—probably more than she even knew—and now was the time to put it all into practice. This time she'd be going without the "training wheels"—without the supervision of Bishop or Malloy or Crane, without the unearned respect that the town seemed to afford its trainees, and most of all . . . without Catherine or Will by her side. This was her show now and hers alone. And she had no intention of screwing it up.

She made sure her badge was strapped to her belt, and then she pulled her gun from the glove compartment, ignoring the slight hitch in her chest that still accompanied the sight of a firearm. Her traumatic history with guns was becoming a little more manageable with each passing day of training. She checked the cartridge and then secured the gun in the holster under her black jacket. She took one last deep breath and then climbed out of the car, slamming the door behind her and locking it with the key chain remote.

Her approach was quick and deliberate: through the garbage-strewn "lawn," up the creaky wooden steps of the empty porch, and straight to the boarded-up door. She gave the door three stiff knocks and then stepped closer to listen for movement. Nothing. Four more knocks yielded the same result. Pure unadulterated silence.

She stepped over to the window and tried to peer through the one pane of glass that had not turned completely opaque with dirt, but all she could see was darkness. The mailbox was nameless, empty, and gathering dust.

This house was positively dead. Just an abandoned hospital-blue box in the middle of nowhere. Standing there on the creaky porch, Gaia finally took a moment to ask herself the obvious question:

What the hell could this decrepit shack on the outskirts of Baltimore possibly have to do with Catherine Sanders?

She stood there puzzled for another few seconds, but the inertia made her twitch with frustration. She hadn't come all this way to find a dead end. She needed more information. She needed to know the deal with this house. Did someone actually live here? Had anyone *ever* lived here? She scanned the adjacent houses for neighbors, but each place looked deader than the last. And then finally, a few houses down and across the street, she saw the first signs of life on Cherry Lane.

There was a diner. Moscone's. Old and dilapidated to be sure, but open for business. And old was good. Someone in there had to know something about this house. Whatever freak had lived here must have stopped in at least once or twice for a cup of coffee and a slice of pie.

There were still a few irrefutable facts in life, and Gaia had yet to see this one disproved: It didn't matter if it was Moscone's in the crap section of Baltimore or Cozy Soup 'n' Burger in the heart of downtown New York. At one point or another, everyone needed a cup of coffee and a slice of pie.

unwelcome attack of
self-consciousness

As Gaia moved toward the diner, the *stillness* hit her again. It was so painfully quiet on this wide, deserted street. The asphalt was cracked and stained, and a paper cup was rolling in the dark gutter near a broken iron drain cover. MOSCONE'S DINER was hand-painted over a dark metal door with dirty glass inlays. A white do-it-yourself sign with attached black letters in the window read, LUNCH SPECIAL: SOUP & SANDWICH, $3.95; FREE COFFEE 12–2. Gaia stepped deliberately forward and pushed on the diner's door, the overhead bell rattling as it swung inward.

The smell of cooking grease entered her nostrils immediately. By comparison, the Greek diners in Manhattan, where she'd scarfed down chocolate milk shakes most of her life, smelled like four-star restaurants. Ignoring the odor, still holding the door open, Gaia waited for her eyes to adjust to the gloom.

Everyone was looking at her.

Control the scene, Agent Crane had told them all in one of his training lectures. Gaia could hear his harsh voice as if he were standing right in front of her, glaring at the FBI class. *Most people have never seen an FBI agent. When they do, they'll want to trust you,* want *to believe in you—so don't make it hard for them.*

Control the scene.

The diner was about half full. There were booths against the big picture windows—they had leather benches repaired with tape—and Formica tables with metal edges. All of them were occupied. An elderly couple in windbreakers with identical bowls of soup sat closest to the door. The man was twisted around in his chair so that he could get a better view of the alien blond thing that had just walked in.

In front of her was a long, low lunch counter. The wall behind it was covered in metal sheets; stacks of miniature cereal boxes leaned against it. A dark-haired man in a clean white T-shirt was frozen in the act of wiping the counter. The chrome stools were occupied by big men with beards and dark caps pulled over their eyes—they looked like truckers. In the far back of the diner, next to what had to be a bathroom door, a thin, unshaven middle-aged man in a dark suit and tie sat motionless at a table, a steaming cup of coffee in front of him, watching her.

Well, Gaia told herself hotly, *you've got their attention. That's step one. Now do something with it.*

A waitress was standing in the middle of the diner, the weak fluorescent overhead light reflecting in her yellow hair. She was not a young woman. Her eyes were heavily mascaraed, and her hands were wrinkled and covered in rings. She had been writing on an order pad and was rooted to the spot, her hand stilled. The young woman at the table in front of her had a small dog in a pink plastic bag. Even the dog was staring at Gaia.

"Hi," Gaia said, giving what she hoped was a disarming smile. With her left hand, she'd already flipped out her badge. "Have you got a second, ma'am? FBI."

Everyone in the diner had a second. You could have heard a pin drop.

That sounded weird, Gaia thought. But this was very different from Virginia. In Quantico, even in the town proper, people were used to the presence of the FBI. When Gaia, Catherine, Will, or whoever walked into a place, people looked up, mildly curious, and went back to whatever they were doing. "Just those government kids," people would tell each other. Suddenly Gaia felt very far away from home.

Had she sounded weird? She couldn't tell. She was supposed to say her name, followed by "FBI," while holding out her badge. It was routine. But somehow, in this silent, dark restaurant, with the deserted, bare street outside the dirty plate-glass window, it was different. This was the real world—and her instincts told her to be unforced and casual.

And don't worry about it, Gaia told herself angrily. She had enough to worry about without this completely unwelcome attack of self-consciousness. It didn't matter if she sounded weird—the important thing was her investigation, how she "controlled the scene."

"Help you with something?" the waitress drawled. Up close, Gaia could see the deep lines in her face and smell the tobacco smoke on her breath. She didn't sound *disrespectful*, exactly. She just wasn't going to give that much deference to a twenty-year-old girl with a mess of unwashed blond hair tied up in a scraggly ponytail—FBI or no.

"If you wouldn't mind," Gaia went on, reaching into her pocket to pull out Catherine's photo, "could you take a good look at this picture, please? Have you ever seen this woman?"

The waitress tore her eyes away from the inside of Gaia's jacket—she must have caught a glimpse of her gun—and turned back to the snapshot Gaia was holding out. It wasn't a particularly good picture—Lyle had found it on the network and quickly printed it out for her before she left. It was a low-resolution digital snapshot of Catherine, taken during the Quantico admissions process. It couldn't have been more than six months old, but to Gaia, Catherine looked years younger. Her hair was already trimmed in her trademark pixie cut (copied from Special Agent Jennifer Bishop), and her smile was innocent and engaging.

"Arf! Arf!" The little dog in the seated woman's pink plastic bag suddenly exploded into a barking fit, its marble-black eyes fixed on Gaia. The sound was deafening.

"Waffles, hush," the woman told her dog. "Sorry, ma'am."

"That's okay," Gaia said, smiling at her. The *ma'am* reassured her—she had control of the room. She hadn't flinched—people might have noticed that. Gaia held the photograph out again.

As the waitress peered skeptically at the snapshot, Gaia tried to stay focused. But it was hard. She couldn't shake the thoughts of Catherine from her head. She *had* to know where Catherine was now—whether she was still smiling, or whether she was trembling and pale, locked in a cold basement room somewhere, shivering.

Or dead, Gaia thought. *Don't forget Malloy's theory.*

"Sorry." The waitress shook her head.

"Are you sure?" Gaia raised her eyebrows. "Ever? Anywhere? Take your time—look at the picture as long as you want."

"I could look at it all day—it won't change the fact that I never seen this girl," the waitress blandly insisted.

The thin man in the black suit was watching her. His eyes seemed to light up in the darkness from the back of the diner. His narrow tie was clipped to his shirt, and his collar was freshly starched. His salt-and-pepper hair reminded Gaia, suddenly, of her father, for reasons she didn't quite understand—the man looked nothing like her father. But his calm stare was different from the gazes of the other patrons—he was coolly appraising her, as if he saw this kind of thing every day and was ready to tell her what she was doing wrong.

"This is a federal investigation," Gaia said loudly, looking around the room. Fourteen pairs of eyes stared back. Her voice echoed against the walls, sounding high-pitched and young. "I'm looking for a missing person—a young woman my age, with short black hair and glasses. Her name is Catherine Saunders."

Who are you kidding? Gaia asked herself. *They can see right through you. Because this* isn't *a "federal investigation"; it's a private wild-goose chase.*

"Waffles," the woman with the pink bag scolded her dog again. The dog had erupted into another frenzied spasm of barking.

"Let me see that photo," the man behind the counter said meekly. Gaia walked over, her heels clicking on the linoleum, and held out the snapshot. The counterman leaned over, squinting critically as he stared at the picture.

"She could look different," Gaia told him. "She could have different hair, or she could have lost her glasses."

Or she could be dead, that same voice repeated maddeningly in her head. The bloodstained duffel bag snapped into focus in her imagination.

"Sorry, ma'am," the counterman said finally, standing back upright. "Can't help you."

"Do you know who lives across the street?"

One of the men at the counter looked over at her. Gaia caught his eye, and the burly man held her steady gaze. Behind him, out the window, the sagging facade of the house faced the street like an empty mask.

"You, sir?" Gaia stepped forward. "Do you know whose house that is?"

"Who wants to know?"

"I told you," Gaia said, moving closer to the man. "I'm a federal agent. If you know who lives over there, I want you to—"

"Little girl like you? I don't believe it," the man said. From up close, his breath smelled of pepper and coffee. He was staring at Gaia, his teeth shining, his unshaven face twisted into a smirk. "Why don't you run home to your mama and leave us alone?"

Gaia reached out and grabbed the man's wrist. Slowly she started bending it downward. The man tried to pull away—looking very surprised when he wasn't able to.

"You interrupted me," Gaia said, leaning closer. "Please don't do that again."

"Let go—"

Gaia held up the photograph. "I want to know if you've seen this woman," she said calmly. "Why don't you take a nice long look and tell me if you recognize her?"

"Let go of my arm!" the man yelled. He was squirming in his seat, but Gaia was holding him at a particular angle so that he couldn't move. "Let me go, damn it!"

"You're not looking," Gaia said, moving the picture closer to his face. "Tell me if the woman in this p—"

"No! No! I've never seen her!" the man yelled out. Everyone in the diner was watching. "I don't know who she is!"

"None of us know," the elderly man in the window booth called out. "Now leave Jimmy alone and let us eat our lunch."

Gaia looked over at the man who'd spoken. He was ladling a spoonful of soup toward his craggy mouth, unconcerned. It was almost like a signal—the clinking of silverware resumed. It was as if the old man had given everyone permission to ignore Gaia.

At the back of the restaurant, the thin man in the black suit watched her curiously. It was almost as if he were waiting to see what she'd do next—how good her training or her instincts were. She quickly moved her eyes away from his and gazed around again at the diner customers.

They don't know anything.

Gaia was suddenly sure of it. They hadn't seen Catherine, and they didn't know who lived across the street—if anyone did. They weren't hiding anything; they just didn't know the answers to her questions. Nodding once, although nobody was watching anymore, Gaia moved toward the door. The bell rang again, weakly, as she walked back out into the still Baltimore air.

Gaia could feel eyes on the back of her neck as she came back out to the sidewalk. She didn't turn around, but she was pretty sure the waitress and the other diner patrons were still watching her.

And the man in the suit.

Gaia wasn't sure what it was about that man that had caught her attention. And she wasn't about to go back for another look. She'd had just about enough of Moscone's Diner and its singularly unhelpful patrons. And all that man had done was sit in the shadows and watch her. Nothing so unusual about that.

Except that she knew better. One thing Gaia had learned from even the rudimentary amount of FBI training she'd had was that you had to pay attention to your instincts. Not *trust* them necessarily (in fact, that could be a terrible mistake) but at least be aware of them. And something about the tall, gaunt man in the diner was sticking with her. *Blue eyes,* she told herself. *Close-cropped salt-and-pepper hair. Not a military cut—a little longer. Needed a shave. Clothes had seen better days—suit a bit wrinkled, white shirt a bit yellowed, collar unstarched.*

Anything else?

Like Dad, Gaia realized. The thought gave her a strange pang. She hadn't seen her father since graduation day at Stanford—

since that unforgettable afternoon when this whole crazy thing had started, the day she'd taken a high dive off a campus roof and saved three hundred people from ten pounds of exploding C-4 plastique. *The guy in the diner reminds me of my father, that's all. Dad, if things had never gone his way—if he'd gotten down on his luck and never quite bounced back.*

That had to be all.

Standing beneath the bleak white sky, Gaia gazed at the house. It was her next stop, obviously. Her only choice was to go back to the diner and question the patrons more thoroughly.

Unfortunately, nothing had changed in the few minutes she'd been across the street. The door was still shut tight, and the house was still silent and unmoving.

So is Catherine in there or not?

Craning her neck, Gaia looked straight overhead. Squinting into the sky, she could see the rusted-out wires running from a nearby phone pole and over to an ancient-looking metal box attached just beneath the house's cracked eaves.

The telephone line.

That's got to be it, she told herself. *That's got to be the line that leads to the mystery modem.* She still couldn't quite believe it, but Lyle had sounded so sure.

Facing the creaky porch steps again, Gaia was very conscious that she was wasting time. She kept fighting off images of Catherine bound and gagged somewhere in the darkness behind that door, waiting for Gaia to stop playing games and come get her. Looking at the front door's rusty doorknob, she knew she could break the door down with one good shove, but there was the little problem of federal law—the law that said she couldn't enter this house without an invitation or a search warrant. And a search warrant was flat-out impossible—it meant a judge and a hearing and actual FBI authorization, none of which she had. And it meant *time*—at least a day's delay. It was out of the question.

She glanced back over her shoulder. The reflections in the diner window made it impossible to see whether she was being watched—and at this point, the last thing she needed was someone calling the bureau and checking up on her. *A young blond woman was just here,* Gaia imagined the waitress saying into the phone. *Claimed to be FBI—waved a badge but didn't seem to know what she was doing. Then she went across the street and broke into that house.*

Casually, as if she were taking a scenic walk, Gaia strolled to the left, heading across the dirt yard and around the side of the house. Her footsteps sank into the soft ground as she walked. Brushing a stray strand of hair from her face, she snuck a glance back at the diner and the sidewalk. Nothing. Nobody around. She kept going, and once she was out of view of the street, she reached under her jacket and pulled out her gun.

The weeds got higher as she moved into the shadows behind the house. She could smell the stink of garbage getting stronger. Without looking down, she could tell she was walking on old beer cans and God knew what else in those tall weeds. The garbage smell grew stronger still, and Gaia could see why. Black plastic trash bags were strewn everywhere.

She tried not to think about what could be hidden in this disgusting backyard. It would take a team of five agents most of an afternoon to go through a place like this, carefully bagging and tagging everything and collecting chemical and forensic evidence. Gaia remembered a story Agent Crane had told them, about an innocent-looking Idaho housewife who'd had two bodies buried in the icy ground behind her trailer home.

She finally sidled up to the back door, holding her gun straight out in front of her. She tried to stick to procedure, looking around for all her "danger spots"—the spots where she was vulnerable to an attack. There was a laundry line strung with bedsheets over a fence behind her—no sniper spots, no danger areas. Good. In the other direction, she saw dark overhanging trees and more garbage bags—fine. Raising the gun in her right hand, she reached out with her left and rapped on the door.

"Hello?" she called out. "Anybody home?"

Nothing. Her own reflection looked back at her from the cracked glass of the door. She rapped again more loudly.

Her shadow on the door suddenly deepened—a cloud bank had shifted and the sky had darkened. Somewhere in that brief gust of wind, as Gaia held her breath, she swore she'd heard the faintest voice coming from inside the house. *Catherine?* No—it had been a male voice. Very indistinct, and very far away. Probably the television.

Now she was using every ounce of her will to fight off the impulse to break in.

Late at night, in their dorm room, Gaia and Catherine had gone through all the books, memorizing the guidelines for criminal investigation and the rules of evidence. Catherine's memory was impeccable—nearly as good as Gaia's—so they'd made fast work of it. *A federal agent may not enter upon private property,* Gaia recited to herself now, *unless sufficient evidence exists that a criminal act or acts or the reckless endangerment of civilians is in process within said property, such that the agent's intervention is necessary to prevent such crime from occurring or concluding.*

The blurred, faint male voice kept talking inside the house. She could hear it for sure now. It sounded very much like a television—the rapid-fire delivery of a commercial announcer. Now she could hear a female voice too and background music. Definitely a television.

But it could *be a crime in progress,* she convinced herself. *It could be.*

Here goes, she muttered, sighing heavily. With the complete knowledge that she was crossing a line that she couldn't uncross, Gaia pulled back and slammed her shoulder into the door.

With a tremendous crack, the lock fell to the ground and the door swung inward. It gave so quickly that Gaia nearly lost her balance, stumbling forward into the darkness. She kept her grip on the gun, immediately whipping her body to one side, out of the bright doorway, where she knew she presented a perfect target.

As many as 1 in 3 Americans
who have HIV... don't know it.

TAKE CONTROL.
KNOW YOUR STATUS.
GET TESTED.

To learn more about HIV testing,
or get a free guide to HIV and
other sexually transmitted diseases:

www.knowhivaids.org
1-866-344-KNOW

Britney is the girl everyone
loves to hate.

She's **popular, blond,** and **fabulous.**
Sure, people are jealous. . . .

But jealous enough to **want her dead?**

killing britney

A thrilling new novel by Sean Olin

from Simon Pulse • published by Simon & Schuster